ALL FIRES THE FIRE

ALL FIRES

Julio Cortázar

AND OTHER STORIES

Translated from the Spanish by Suzanne Jill Levine

THE FIRE

PANTHEON BOOKS, NEW YORK

Copyright © 1973 by Random House, Inc.

All rights reserved under International and Pan-American Copyright
Conventions. Published in the United States by Pantheon Books,
a division of Random House, Inc., New York, and simultaneously in
Canada by Random House of Canada Limited, Toronto. Originally
published in Buenos Aires as *todos los fuegos el fuego* by Sudamericana
Buenos Aires. Copyright © 1966 by Editorial Sudamericana. Translation
first published in hardcover by Pantheon Books, a division of Random
House, Inc., in 1973.

Assistance for the translation of this book has been given by the Center for
Inter-American Relations.

Library of Congress Cataloging in Publication Data

Cortázar, Julio.
All Fires the Fire and Other Stories
Translation of Todos los fuegos el fuego.
CONTENTS: The southern thruway. —The health
of the sick. —Meeting. —Nurse Cora. [etc.]
I. Title.
PZ3.C81929A13 [PQ7797.C7145]   863   73–2937
ISBN 0-394-75358-5

Design by Kenneth Miyamoto

Manufactured in the United States of America
by Haddon Craftsmen, Scranton, Pennsylvania

First American Paperback Edition

9 8 7 6 5 4 3 2

CONTENTS

The Southern Thruway

Sweltering motorists do not seem to have a history . . . As a reality a traffic jam is impressive, but it doesn't say much.
——*Arrigo Benedetti*, L'Espresso, Rome, 6.21.64

AT FIRST the girl in the Dauphine had insisted on keeping track of the time, but the engineer in the Peugeot 404 didn't care anymore. Anyone could look at his watch, but it was as if that time strapped to your right wrist or the beep beep on the radio were measuring something else—the time of those who haven't made the blunder of trying to return to Paris on the southern thruway on a Sunday afternoon and, just past Fontainebleau, have had to slow down to a crawl, stop, six rows of cars on either side (everyone knows that on Sundays both sides of the thruway are reserved for those returning to the capital), start the engine, move three yards, stop, talk with the two nuns in the 2CV on the right, look in the rear-view mirror at the pale man driving the Caravelle, ironically envy the birdlike contentment of the couple in the Peugeot 203 (behind the girl's Dauphine) playing

The translator wishes to thank Roberto González Echevarría for his collaboration in the translation of this story.

with their little girl, joking, and eating cheese, or suffer the exasperated outbursts of the two boys in the Simca, in front of the Peugeot 404, and even get out at the stops to explore, not wandering off too far (no one knows when the cars up front will start moving again, and you have to run back so that those behind you won't begin their battle of horn blasts and curses), and thus move up along a Taunus in front of the girl's Dauphine—she is still watching the time—and exchange a few discouraged or mocking words with the two men traveling with the little blond boy, whose great joy at this particular moment is running his toy car over the seats and the rear ledge of the Taunus, or to dare and move up just a bit, since it doesn't seem the cars up ahead will budge very soon, and observe with some pity the elderly couple in the ID Citroën that looks like a big purple bathtub with the little old man and woman swimming around inside, he resting his arms on the wheel with an air of resigned fatigue, she nibbling on an apple, fastidious rather than hungry.

By the fourth time he had seen all that, done all that, the engineer decided not to leave his car again and to just wait for the police to somehow dissolve the bottleneck. The August heat mingled with the tire-level temperature and made immobility increasingly irritating. All was gasoline fumes, screechy screams from the boys in the Simca, the sun's glare bouncing off glass and chrome frames, and to top it off, the contradictory sensation of being trapped in a jungle of cars made to run. The engineer's 404 occupied the second lane on the right, counting from the median, which meant that he had four cars on his right and seven on his left, although, in fact, he could see distinctly only the eight cars surrounding him and their occupants, whom he was already tired of observing. He had chatted with them all, except for the boys in the Simca, whom he disliked. Between stops the situation had been discussed down to the smallest detail, and the general impression was that, up to Corbeil-Essonnes, they would move more or less slowly, but that between Corbeil and Juvisy things would pick up once the helicopters and motorcycle police managed to break up the worst of the bottleneck. No one doubted that a serious accident had taken place in the area, which could be the only explanation for such an incredible delay. And with that, the government, taxes, road conditions, one topic after another, three yards, another commonplace, five yards, a sententious phrase or a restrained curse.

The two little nuns in the 2CV wanted so much to get to Milly-la-Forêt before eight because they were bringing a basket of greens for the cook. The couple in the Peugeot 203 were particularly interested in not missing the games on television at nine-thirty; the girl in the Dauphine had told the engineer that she didn't care if she got to Paris a little late, she was complaining only as a matter of principle because she thought it was a crime to subject thousands of people to the discomforts of a camel caravan. In the last few hours (it must have been around five, but the heat was unbearable) they had moved about fifty yards according to the engineer's calculations, but one of the men from the Taunus who had come to talk, bringing his little boy with him, pointed ironically to the top of a solitary plane tree, and the girl in the Dauphine remembered that this plane (if it wasn't a chestnut) had been in line with her car for such a long time that she would no longer bother looking at her watch, since all calculations were useless.

Night would never come; the sun's vibrations on the highway and cars pushed vertigo to the edge of nausea. Dark glasses, handkerchiefs moistened with cologne pressed against foreheads, the measures improvised to protect oneself from screaming reflections or from the foul breath expelled by exhaust pipes at every start, were being organized, perfected, and were the object of reflection and commentary. The engineer got out again to stretch his legs, exchanged a few words with the couple (who looked like farmers) traveling in the Ariane in front of the nun's 2CV. Behind the 2CV was a Volkswagen with a soldier and a girl who looked like newlyweds. The third line toward the edge of the road no longer interested him because he would have had to go dangerously far from the 404; he could distinguish colors, shapes, Mercedes Benz, ID, Lancia, Skoda, Morris Minor, the whole catalog. To the left, on the opposite side of the road, an unreachable jungle of Renaults, Anglias, Peugeots, Porsches, Volvos. It was so monotonous that finally, after chatting with the two men in the Taunus and unsuccessfully trying to exchange views with the solitary driver of the Caravelle, there was nothing better to do than to go back to the 404 and pick up the same conversation about the time, distances, and the movies with the girl in the Dauphine.

Sometimes a stranger would appear, someone coming from the opposite side of the road or from the outside lanes on the right, who would slip between cars to bring some news, probably false, relayed from car to car along the hot miles. The stranger would savor the impact of his news, the slamming of doors as passengers rushed back to comment on the events; but after a while a horn, or an engine starting up, would drive the stranger away, zigzagging through the cars, rushing to get into his and away from the justified anger of the others. And so, all afternoon, they heard about the crash of a Floride and a 2CV near Corbeil—three dead and one child wounded; the double collision of a Fiat 1500 and a Renault station wagon, which in turn smashed into an Austin full of English tourists; the overturning of an Orly airport bus, teeming with passengers from the Copenhagen flight. The engineer was sure that almost everything was

false, although something awful must have happened near
Corbeil or even near Paris itself to have paralyzed traffic to
such an extent. The farmers in the Ariane, who had a farm
near Montereau and knew the region well, told them about
another Sunday when traffic had been at a standstill for five
hours, but even that much time seemed ludicrous now that
the sun, going down on the left side of the road, poured a
last avalanche of orange jelly into each car, making metals
boil and clouding vision, the treetops behind them never
completely disappearing, the shadow barely seen in the distance up ahead never getting near enough so that you could
feel the line of cars was moving, even if only a little, even
if you had to start and then slam on the breaks and never
leave first gear; the dejection of again going from first to
neutral, brake, hand brake, stop, and the same thing time
and time again.

At one point, tired of inactivity, the engineer decided
to take advantage of a particularly endless stop to make a
tour of the lanes on the left and, leaving the Dauphine
behind he found a DKW, another 2CV, a Fiat 600, and he
stopped by a De Soto to chat with an astonished tourist from
Washington, D.C. who barely understood French, but had
to be at the Place de l'Opéra at eight sharp, you understand,
my wife will be awfully anxious, damn it, and they were
talking about things in general when a traveling salesman
type emerged from the DKW to tell them that someone had
come by before saying that a Piper Cub had crashed in the
middle of the highway, several dead. The American couldn't
give a damn about the Piper Cub, likewise the engineer who,
hearing a chorus of horns, rushed back to the 404, passing
on the news as he went to the men in the Taunus and the
couple in the 203. He saved a more detailed account for the
girl in the Dauphine as the cars moved a few slow yards.
(Now the Dauphine was slightly behind in relation to the

404, later it would be the opposite; actually, the twelve rows moved as a block, as if an invisible traffic cop at the end of the highway were ordering them to advance in unison, not letting anyone get ahead.) A Piper Cub, Miss, is a small touring plane. Oh. Some nerve crashing right on the thruway on a Sunday afternoon! Really. If only it weren't so hot in these damn cars, if those trees to the right were finally behind us, if the last number in the odometer were finally to fall into its little black hole instead of hanging by its tail, endlessly.

At one point (night was softly falling, the horizon of car tops was turning purple), a big white butterfly landed on the Dauphine's windshield, and the girl and the engineer admired its wings, spread in brief and perfect suspension while it rested; then with acute nostalgia, they watched it fly away over the Taunus and the old couple's ID, head toward the Simca, where a hunter's hand tried vainly to catch it, wing amiably over the Ariane, where the two farmers seemed to be eating something, and finally disappear to the right. At dusk, the line of cars made a first big move of about forty yards; when the engineer looked absently at the odometer, one half of the six had vanished, and the seven was beginning to move down. Almost everybody listened to the radio, and the boys in the Simca had theirs at full blast, singing along with a twist, rocking the car with their gyrations; the nuns were saying their rosaries; the little boy in the Taunus had fallen asleep with his face against the window, the toy car still in his hand. At one point (it was nighttime now), some strangers came with more news, as contradictory as the news already forgotten. It wasn't a Piper, but a glider flown by a general's daughter. It was true that a Renault van had smashed into an Austin, not in Juvisy though, but practically at the gates of Paris. One of the strangers explained to the couple in the 203 that the pavement had caved in around

Igny, and five cars had overturned when their front wheels got caught in the cracks. The idea of a natural catastrophe spread all the way to the engineer, who shrugged without a comment. Later, thinking of those first few hours of darkness when they had begun to breathe more easily, he remembered that, at one point, he had stuck his arm out of his window to tap on the Dauphine and wake up the girl; she had fallen asleep, oblivious to a new advance. It was perhaps already midnight when one of the nuns timidly offered him a ham sandwich, assuming that he was hungry. The engineer accepted it (although, in fact, he felt nauseous) and asked if he could share it with the girl in the Dauphine, who accepted and voraciously ate the sandwich and a chocolate bar she got from the traveling salesman in the DKW, her neighbor to the left. A lot of people had stepped out of the stuffy cars, because again it had been hours since the last advance; thirst was prevalent, the bottles of lemonade and even the wine on board were already exhausted. The first to complain was the little girl in the 203, and the soldier and the engineer left their cars to go with her father to get water. In front of the Simca, where the radio seemed to provide ample nourishment, the engineer found a Beaulieu occupied by an older woman with nervous eyes. No, she didn't have any water, but she could give him some candy for the little girl. The couple in the ID consulted each other briefly before the old woman pulled a small can of fruit juice out of her bag. The engineer expressed his gratitude and asked if they were hungry, or if he could be of any service; the old man shook his head, but the old lady seemed to accept his offer silently. Later, the girl from the Dauphine and the engineer explored the rows on the left, without going too far; they came back with a few pastries and gave them to the old lady in the ID, just in time to run back to their own cars under a shower of horn blasts.

Aside from those quick jaunts, there was so little to do that the hours began to blend together, becoming one in the memory; at one point, the engineer thought of striking that day from his appointments book and had to keep from laughing out loud, but later, when the nuns, the men in the Taunus, and the girl in the Dauphine began to make contradictory calculations, he realized it would have been better to keep track of time. The local radio stations stopped transmitting for the day, and only the traveling salesman had a short-wave radio, which insisted on reporting exclusively on the stockmarket. Around three, it seemed as if a tacit agreement had been reached, and the line didn't move until dawn. The boys in the Simca pulled out inflatable beds and laid down by their car; the engineer lowered the back of the front seat of the 404 and offered the cushions to the nuns, who refused them; before lying down for a while, the engineer thought of the girl in the Dauphine, who was still at the wheel, and, pretending it didn't make any difference to him, offered to switch cars with her until dawn, but she refused, claiming that she could sleep fine in any position. For a while, you could hear the boy in the Taunus cry; he was lying on the back seat and probably suffering from the heat. The nuns were still praying when the engineer laid down on the seat and began falling asleep, but his sleep was too close to wakefulness, and he finally awoke sweaty and nervous, not realizing at first where he was. Sitting up straight, he began to perceive confused movements outside, a gliding of shadows between the cars, and then he saw a black bulk disappear toward the edge of the highway; he guessed why, and later he, too, left his car to relieve himself at the edge of the road; there were no hedges or trees, only the starless black fields, something that looked like an abstract wall fencing off the white strip of asphalt with its motionless river of cars. He almost bumped into the farmer from the Ariane, who mumbled something unintelligible; the smell of gasoline over the road now mingled with the more acid presence of man, and the engineer hurried back to his car as soon as he could. The girl in the Dauphine slept leaning on the steering wheel, a lock of hair in her eyes. Before climbing into the 404, the engineer amused himself by watching her shadow, divining the curve of her slightly puckered lips. On the other side, smoking silently, the man in the DKW was also watching the girl sleep.

In the morning they moved a little, enough to give them hope that by afternoon the route to Paris would open up. At nine, a stranger brought good news: The cracks on the road had been filled, and traffic would soon be back to normal. The boys in the Simca turned on the radio, and one of them climbed on top of the car singing and shouting. The engineer told himself that the news was as false as last night's and that the stranger had taken advantage of the group's happiness to ask for and get an orange from the couple in the Ariane. Later another stranger came and tried the same trick, but got nothing. The heat was beginning to rise, and the people preferred to stay in their cars and wait for the good news to come true. At noon, the little girl in the 203 began crying again, and the girl in the Dauphine went to play with her and made friends with her parents. The 203's had no luck: On the right they had the silent man in the Caravelle, oblivious to everything happening around him, and from their left they had to endure the verbose indignation of the driver of the Floride, for whom the bottleneck was a personal affront. When the little girl complained of thirst again, the engineer decided to talk to the couple in the Ariane, convinced that there were many provisions in that car. To his surprise, the farmers were very friendly; they realized that in a situation like this it was necessary to help one another, and they thought that if someone took charge of the group (the woman made a circular gesture with her hand, encompassing the dozen cars surrounding them), they would have enough to get them to Paris. The idea of appointing himself organizer bothered him, and he chose to call the men from the Taunus for a meeting with the couple in the Ariane. A while later, the rest of the group was consulted one by one. The young soldier in the Volkswagen agreed immediately, and the couple in the 203 offered the few provisions they had left. (The girl in the Dauphine had gotten a glass of pomegranate juice for the little girl, who was now laughing and playing.) One of the Taunus men who went to consult with the boys in the Simca received only mocking consent; the pale man in the Caravelle said it made no difference to him, they could do whatever they wanted. The old couple in the ID and the lady in the Beaulieu reacted with visible joy, as if they felt more protected now. The drivers of the Floride and DKW made no comment, and the American looked at them astonished, saying something about God's will. The engineer found it easy to nominate one of the Taunus men, in whom he had instinctive confidence, as coordinator of all activities. No one would have to go hungry for the time being, but they needed water; the leader, whom the boys in the Simca called Taunus for fun, asked the engineer, the soldier, and one of the boys to explore the zone of highway around them, offering food in exchange for beverages. Taunus, who evidently knew how to command, figured that they should obtain supplies for a maximum of a day and a half, taking the most pessimistic view. In the nun's 2CV and the farmer's Ariane there were enough supplies for such a period of time and, if the explorers returned with water, all problems would be solved. But only the soldier returned with a full flask, and its owner had demanded food for two people in exchange. The engineer failed to find anyone who could give him water, but his trip allowed him to observe that beyond his group other cells were being organized and were facing similar problems; at a given moment, the driver of an Alfa Romeo refused to speak to him, referring him to the leader of his group five cars behind. Later, the boy from the Simca came back without any water, but Taunus figured they already had enough water for the two children, the old lady in the ID, and the rest of the women. The engineer was telling the girl in the Dauphine about his trip around the periphery (it was one in the afternoon, and the sun kept them in their cars), when she interrupted him with a gesture and pointed to the Simca. In two leaps the engineer reached the car and grabbed the elbow of the boy sprawled in the seat and drinking in great gulps from a flask he had brought back hidden in his jacket. To the boy's angry gesture the engineer responded by increasing the pressure on his arm; the other boy got out of the car and jumped on the engineer, who took two steps back and waited for him, almost with pity. The soldier was already running toward them, and the nuns' shrieks alerted Taunus and his companion. Taunus listened to what had happened, approached the boy with the flask, and slapped him twice. Sobbing, the boy screamed and protested, while the other grumbled without daring to intervene. The engineer took the flask away and gave it to Taunus. Horns began to blare, and everyone returned to his car, but to no avail, since the line moved barely five yards.

At siesta time, under a sun that was even stronger than the day before, one of the nuns took off her coif, and her companion doused her temples with cologne. The women improvised their Samaritan activities little by little, moving from one car to the next, taking care of the children to allow the men more freedom. No one complained, but the jokes were strained, always based on the same word plays, in snobbish skepticism. The greatest humiliation for the girl in the Dauphine and the engineer was to feel sweaty and dirty; the farmers' absolute indifference to the odor that emanated from their armpits moved them to pity. Toward dusk, the engineer looked casually into the rear-view mirror and found, as always, the pale face and tense features of the driver of the Caravelle who, like the fat driver of the Floride, had remained aloof from all the activities. He thought that his features had become sharper and wondered if he were sick. But later on, when he went to talk with the soldier and his wife, he had a chance to look at him more closely and told himself that the man was not sick, that it was something else, a separation, to give it a name. The soldier in the Volkswagen later told him that his wife was afraid of that silent man who never left the wheel and seemed to sleep awake. Conjectures arose; a folklore was created to fight against inactivity. The children in the Taunus and the 203 had become friends, quarreled, and later made up; their parents visited each other, and once in a while the girl in the Dauphine went to see how the old lady in the ID and the woman in the Beaulieu were doing. At dusk, when some gusts of wind swept through, and the sun went behind the clouds in the west, the people were happy, thinking it would get cooler. A few drops fell, coinciding with an extraordinary advance of almost 100 yards; far away, lightning glowed, and it got even hotter. There was so much electricity in the atmosphere that Taunus, with an instinct the engineer silently admired, left the group alone until night, as if he sensed the possible consequences of the heat and fatigue. At eight, the women took charge of distributing the food; it had been decided that the farmer's Ariane should be the general warehouse and the nun's 2CV a supplementary depot. Taunus had gone in person to confer with the leaders of the four or five neighboring groups; later, with the help of the soldier and the man in the 203, he took an amount of food to the other groups and returned with more water and some wine. It was decided that the boys in the Simca would yield their inflatable beds to the old lady in the ID and the woman in the Beaulieu; the girl in the Dauphine also brought them two plaid blankets, and the engineer offered his car, which he mockingly called the "sleeping car," to whomever might need it. To his surprise, the girl in the Dauphine accepted the offer and that night shared the 404 cushions with one of the nuns; the other nun went to sleep in the 203 with the little girl and her mother, while the husband spent the night on the pavement wrapped in a blanket. The engineer was not sleepy and played dice with Taunus and his mate; at one point, the farmer in the Ariane joined them, and they talked about politics and drank a few shots of brandy that the farmer had turned over to Taunus that morning. The night wasn't bad; it had cooled down, and a few stars shone between the clouds.

Toward morning, they were overcome by sleep, that need to feel covered which came with the half-light of dawn. While Taunus slept beside the boy in the back seat, his friend and the engineer rested up front. Between two images of a dream, the engineer thought he heard screams in the distance and saw a vague glow; the leader of another group came to tell them that thirty cars ahead there had been the beginnings of a fire in an Estafette—someone had tried to boil vegetables on the sly. Taunus joked about the incident as he went from car to car to find out how they had spent the night, but everyone got his message. That morning, the line began to move very early, and there was an excited rush to pick up mattresses and blankets, but, since the same was probably happening all over, almost no one was impatient or blew his horn. Toward noon, they had moved more than fifty yards, and the shadow of a forest could be seen to the right of the highway. They envied those lucky people who at that moment could go to the shoulder of the road and enjoy the shade; maybe there was a brook or a faucet with running water. The girl in the Dauphine closed her eyes and thought of a shower falling down her neck and back, running down her legs; the engineer, observing her out of the corner of his eye, saw two tears streaming down her cheeks.

Taunus, who had moved up to the ID, came back to get the younger women to tend the old lady, who wasn't feeling well. The leader of the third group to the rear had a doctor among his men, and the soldier rushed to get him. The engineer, who had followed with ironical benevolence the efforts the boys in the Simca had been making to be forgiven, thought it was time to give them their chance. With the pieces of a tent the boys covered the windows of the 404, and the "sleeping car" became an ambulance where the old lady could sleep in relative darkness. Her husband lay down beside her, and everyone left them alone with the doctor. Later, the nuns attended to the old lady, who felt much better, and the engineer spent the afternoon as best he could, visiting other cars and resting in Taunus' when the sun bore down too hard; he had to run only three times to his car, where the old couple seemed to sleep, to move it up with the line to the next stop. Night came without their having made it to the forest.

Toward two in the morning, the temperature dropped, and those who had blankets were glad to bundle up. Since the line couldn't move until morning (it was something you felt in the air, that came from the horizon of motionless cars in the night), the engineer sat down to smoke with Taunus and to chat with the farmer in the Ariane and the soldier. Taunus' calculations no longer corresponded to reality, and he said so frankly; something would have to be done in the morning to get more provisions and water. The soldier went to get the leaders of the neighboring groups, who were not sleeping either, and they discussed the problem quietly so as not to wake up the women. The leaders had spoken with the leaders of faraway groups, in a radius of about eighty or 100 cars, and they were sure that the situation was analogous everywhere. The farmer knew the region well and proposed that two or three men from each group go out at dawn to buy provisions from the neighboring farms, while Taunus appointed drivers for the cars left unattended during the expedition. The idea was good, and it was not difficult to collect money from those present; it was decided that the farmer, the soldier, and Taunus' friend would go together, taking all the paper bags, string bags, and flasks available. The other leaders went back to their groups to organize similar expeditions and, at dawn, the situation was explained to the women, and the necessary preparations were made, so that the line could keep moving. The girl in the Dauphine told the engineer that the old lady felt better already and insisted on going back to her ID; at eight, the doctor came and saw no reason why the couple shouldn't return to their car. In any case, Taunus decided that the 404 would be the official ambulance; for fun the boys made a banner with a red cross and put it on the antenna. For a while now, people preferred to leave their cars as little as possible; the temperature continued to drop, and at noon, showers began to fall with lightning in the distance. The farmer's wife rushed to gather water with a funnel and a plastic pitcher, to the special amusement of the boys in the Simca. Watching all this, leaning on his wheel with a book in front of him that he wasn't too interested in, the engineer wondered why the expeditionaries were taking so long; later, Taunus discreetly called him over to his car and, when they got in, told him they had failed. Taunus' friend gave details: The farms were either abandoned or the people refused to sell to them, alleging regulations forbidding the sale to private individuals and suspecting that they were inspectors taking advantage of the circumstances to test them. In spite of everything, they had been able to bring back a small amount of water and some provisions, perhaps stolen by the soldier, who was grinning and not going into details. Of course, the bottleneck couldn't last much longer, but the food they had wasn't the best for the children or the old lady. The doctor, who came around four-thirty to see the sick woman, made a gesture of weariness and exasperation and told Taunus that the same thing was happening in all the neighboring groups. The radio had spoken about emergency measures being taken to clear up the thruway, but aside from a helicopter that appeared briefly at dusk, there was no action to be seen. At any rate, the heat was gradually tapering off, and people seemed to be waiting for night to cover up in their blankets and erase a few more hours of waiting in their sleep. From his car the engineer listened to the conversation between the girl in the Dauphine and the traveling salesman in the DKW, who was telling her jokes that made her laugh halfheartedly. He was surprised to see the lady from the Beaulieu, who never left her car, and got out to see if she needed something, but she only wanted the latest news and went over to talk with the nuns. A nameless tedium weighed upon them at nightfall; people expected more from sleep than from the always contradictory or unfounded news. Taunus' friend discreetly went to get the engineer, the soldier, and the man in the 203. Taunus informed them that the man in the Floride had just deserted; one of the boys in the Simca had seen the car empty and after a while started looking for the man just to kill time. No one knew the fat man in the Floride well. He had complained a lot the first day, but had turned out to be as silent as the driver of the Caravelle. When at five in the morning there was no longer any doubt that Floride, as the boys in the Simca got a kick out of calling him, had deserted, taking a handbag with him and leaving behind another filled with shirts and underwear, Taunus decided that one of the boys would take charge of the abandoned car so as not to immobilize the lane. They were all vaguely annoyed by this desertion in the dark and wondered how far Floride could have gotten in his flight through the fields. Aside from this, it seemed to be the night for big decisions; lying on the seat cushion of his 404, the engineer seemed to hear a moan, but he figured it was coming from the soldier and his wife, which, after all, was understandable in the middle of the night and under such circumstances. But then he thought better and lifted the canvas that covered the rear window; by the light of one of the few stars shining, he saw the ever-present windshield of the Caravelle a yard and a half away, and behind it, as if glued to the glass and slightly slanted, the man's convulsed face. Quietly, he got out the left side so as not to wake up the nuns and approached the Caravelle. Then he looked for Taunus, and the soldier went to get the doctor. Obviously, the man had committed suicide by taking some kind of poison; a few lines scrawled in pencil in his appointments book were enough, plus the letter addressed to one Yvette, someone who had left him in Vierzon. Fortunately, the habit of sleeping in the cars was well established (the nights were so cold now that no one would have thought of staying outside), and few were bothered by others slipping between the cars toward the edges of the thruway to relieve themselves. Taunus called a war council, and the doctor agreed with his proposal. To leave the body on the edge of the road would mean to subject those coming behind to an at least painful surprise; to carry him further out into the fields could provoke a violent reaction from the villagers who, the night before, had threatened and beaten up a boy from another group, out looking for food. The farmer in the Ariane and the traveling salesman had what was needed to hermetically seal the Caravelle's trunk. The girl in the Dauphine joined them just as they were beginning their task, and hung on to the engineer's arm. He quietly explained what had happened and returned her, a little calmer, to her car. Taunus and his men had put the body in the trunk, and the traveling salesman worked with tubes of glue and Scotch tape by the light of the soldier's lantern. Since the woman in the 203 could drive, Taunus decided that her husband would take over the Caravelle, which was on the 203's right; so, in the morning, the little girl in the 203 discovered that her daddy had another car and played for hours at switching cars and putting some of her toys in the Caravelle.

For the first time, it felt cold during the day, and no one thought of taking off his coat. The girl in the Dauphine and the nuns made an inventory of coats available in the group. There were a few sweaters that turned up unexpectedly in the cars, or in some suitcase, a few blankets, a light overcoat or two. A list of priorities was drawn up, and the coats were distributed. Water was again scarce, and Taunus' sent three of his men, including the engineer, to try to establish contact with the villagers. While impossible to say why, outside resistance was total. It was enough to step out of the thruway's boundaries for stones to come raining in from somewhere. In the middle of the night, someone threw a sickle that hit the top of the DKW and fell beside the Dauphine. The traveling salesman turned very pale and didn't move from his car, but the American in the De Soto (who was not in Taunus' group, but was appreciated by everyone for his guffaws and good humor) came running, twirled the sickle around and hurled it back with everything he had, shouting curse words. But Taunus did not think it wise to increase the hostility; perhaps it was still possible to make a trip for water.

Nobody kept track anymore of how much they had moved in that day or days; the girl in the Dauphine thought that it was between eighty and two hundred yards; the engineer was not as optimistic, but amused himself by prolonging and confusing his neighbor's calculations, interested in stealing her away from the traveling salesman, who was courting her in his professional manner. That same afternoon, the boy in charge of the Floride came to tell Taunus that a Ford Mercury was offering water at a good price. Taunus refused, but at nightfall one of the nuns asked the engineer for a drink of water for the old lady in the ID, who was suffering in silence, still holding her husband's hand, and being tended alternately by the nuns and the girl in the Dauphine. There was half a bottle of water left, and the women assigned it to the old lady and the woman in the Beaulieu. That same night Taunus paid out of his own pocket for two bottles of water; the Ford Mercury promised to get more the next day, at double the price.

It was difficult to get together and talk, because it was so cold that no one would leave his car except for very pressing reasons. The batteries were beginning to run down, and they couldn't keep the heaters running all the time, so Taunus decided to reserve the two best equipped cars for the sick, should the situation arise. Wrapped in blankets (the boys in the Simca had ripped off the inside covers of their car to make coats and hats for themselves, and others started to imitate them), everyone tried his best to open doors as little as possible to preserve the heat. On one of those freezing nights the engineer heard the girl in the Dauphine sobbing softly. Quietly he opened her door and groped for her in the dark until he felt a wet cheek. Almost without resistance, she let herself be drawn to the 404; the engineer helped her lie down on the back seat, covered her with his only blanket, and then with his overcoat. Darkness was thicker in the ambulance car, its windows covered with the tent's canvas. At one point, the engineer pulled down the two sun visors and hung his shirt and a sweater from them to shut the car off completely. Toward dawn, she whispered in his ear that before starting to cry she thought she saw in the distance, on the right, the lights of a city.

Maybe it was a city, but in the morning mist you couldn't see more than twenty yards away. Curiously, the line moved a lot more that day, perhaps two or three hundred yards. This coincided with new radio flashes. (Hardly anyone listened anymore, with the exception of Taunus, who felt it was his duty to keep up.) The announcers talked emphatically about exceptional measures that would clear the thruway and referred to the weary toil of highway patrolmen and police forces. Suddenly, one of the nuns became delirious. As her companion looked on terrified, and the girl in the Dauphine dabbed her temples with what was left of the cologne, the nun spoke of Armageddon, the Ninth Day, the chain of cinnabar. The doctor came much later, making his way through the snow that had been falling since noon and that was gradually walling the cars in. He regretted the lack of sedatives and advised them to put the nun in a car with good heating. Taunus put her in his own car, and the little boy moved to the Caravelle with his little girl friend from the 203; they played with their toy cars and had a lot of fun, because they were the only ones who didn't go hungry. That day and the following days, it snowed almost continuously, and when the line moved up a few yards, the snow that had accumulated between cars had to be removed by improvised means.

No one would have conceived of being surprised at the way they were getting provisions and water. The only thing Taunus could do was administer the common fund and get as much as possible out of trades. The Ford Mercury and a

Porsche came every night to traffic with food; Taunus and the engineer were in charge of distributing it according to the physical state of each one. Incredibly, the old lady in the ID was surviving, although sunken in a stupor that the women diligently fought off. The lady in the Beaulieu, who had been fainting and feeling nauseous a few days before, had recovered with the cold weather and was now one of the most active in helping the nun take care of her companion, still weak and a bit lost. The soldier's wife and 203's were in charge of the two children; the traveling salesman in the DKW, perhaps to console himself for losing Dauphine to the engineer, spent hours telling stories to the children. At night, the groups entered another life, secret and private; doors would open or close to let a frozen figure in or out; no one looked at the others; eyes were as blind as darkness itself. Some kind of happiness endured here and there under dirty blankets, in hands with overgrown fingernails, in bodies smelling of unchanged clothes and of days cramped inside. The girl in the Dauphine had not been mistaken—a city sparkled in the distance, and they were approaching it slowly. In the afternoons, one of the boys in the Simca would climb to the top of the car, relentless lookout wrapped in pieces of seat covers and green burlap. Tired of exploring the futile horizon, he'd look for the thousandth time at the cars surrounding him; somewhat enviously he'd discover Dauphine in 404's car, a hand caressing a neck, the end of a kiss. To play a joke on them, now that he had regained 404's friendship, he'd yell that the line was about to move. Dauphine would have to leave 404 and go to her car, but after a while she'd come back looking for warmth, and the boy in the Simca would have liked so much to bring a girl from another group to his car, but it was unthinkable with this cold and hunger, not to mention that the group up front was openly hostile to Taunus' because of some story about a can of condensed milk, and except for official transactions with Ford Mercury and Porsche, there was no possible contact with other groups. Then the boy in the Simca would sigh unhappily and continue his lookout until the snow and the cold forced him trembling back into his car.

But the cold began to give way and, after a period of rains and winds that enervated a few spirits and increased food supply difficulties, came some cool sunny days when it was again possible to leave your car, pay visits, restore relations with neighboring groups. The leaders had discussed the situation, and peace was finally made with the group ahead. Ford Mercury's sudden disappearance was much talked about, although no one knew what could have happened to him. But Porsche kept coming and controlling the black market. Water and some preserves were never completely lacking, but the group's funds were diminishing, and Taunus and the engineer asked themselves what would happen the day when there was no more money to give Porsche. The possibility of an ambush was brought up, of taking him prisoner and forcing him to reveal the source of his supplies; but the line had advanced a good stretch, and the leaders preferred to wait some more and avoid the risk of ruining it all by a hasty decision. The engineer, who had given into an almost pleasant indifference, was momentarily stunned by the timid news from the girl in the Dauphine, but later he understood that nothing could be done to avoid it, and the idea of having a child by her seemed as natural as the nightly distribution of supplies or the secret trips to the edge of the thruway. Nor could the death of the old lady in the ID surprise anyone. Again it was necessary to work at night, to console her husband, who just couldn't understand, and to keep him company. A fight broke out between the two groups up ahead, and Taunus had to act as mediator and tentatively solve the disagreement. Anything would happen at any moment, without prearranged schedules; the most important thing began when nobody expected it anymore, and the least responsible was the first to find out. Standing on the roof of the Simca, the elated lookout had the impression that the horizon had changed (it was dusk; the meager, level light of a yellowish sun was slipping away) and that something unbelievable was happening five hundred, three hundred, two hundred and fifty yards away. He shouted it to 404, and 404 said something to Dauphine, and she dashed to her car, when Taunus, the soldier, and the farmer were already running, and from the roof of the Simca the boy was pointing ahead and endlessly repeating the news as if to convince himself that what he was seeing was true. Then they heard the rumble, as if a heavy but uncontrollable migratory wave were awakening from a long slumber and testing its strength. Taunus yelled at them to get back to their cars; the Beaulieu, the ID, the Fiat 600, and the De Soto started moving at once. Now the 2CV, the Taunus, the Simca, and the Ariane were beginning to move, and the boy in the Simca, proud of what was to him something of a personal triumph, turned to the 404 and waved his arm, while the 404, the Dauphine, the 2CV, and the DKW in turn started moving. But it all hinged on how long this was going to last, 404 thought almost routinely, as he kept pace with Dauphine and smiled encouragement to her. Behind them, the Volkswagen, the Caravelle, the 203, and the Floride started moving slowly, a stretch in first gear, then second, forever second, but already without having to clutch, as so many times before, with the foot firmly on the accelerator, waiting to move on to third. 404, reaching out to touch Dauphine's hand, barely grazed her fingertips, saw on her face a smile of incredulous hope, and thought that they would make it to Paris and take a bath, go somewhere together, to her house or his to take a bath, eat, bathe endlessly and eat and drink, and that later there would be furniture, a bedroom with furniture and a bathroom with shaving cream to really shave, and toilets, food and toilets and sheets, Paris was a toilet and two sheets and hot water running down his chest and legs, and a nail clipper, and white wine, they would drink white wine before kissing and smell each other's lavender water and cologne before really making love with the lights on, between clean sheets, and bathing again just for fun, to make love and bathe and drink and go to the barber shop, go into the bathroom, caress the sheets and caress each other between the sheets and make love among the suds and lavender water and toothbrushes, before beginning to think about what they were going to do, about the child and all the problems and the future, and all that as long as they didn't stop, just as long as the rows kept on moving, even though you couldn't go to third yet, just moving like that, in second, but moving. With his bumper touching the Simca, 404 leaned back, felt the speed picking up, felt that it was possible to accelerate without bumping into the Simca and that the Simca could accelerate without fear of crashing into Beaulieu, and that behind came the Caravelle and that they all accelerated more and more, and that it was O.K. to move on to third without forcing the engine, and the pace became even, and they all accelerated even more, and 404 looked around with surprise and tenderness, searching for Dauphine's eyes. But, naturally, speeding up like that the lanes could no longer stay parallel. Dauphine had moved almost a yard ahead of 404, and he saw her neck and barely her profile just as she was turning to look at him with surprise, noticing that the 404 was falling further behind. 404 calmed her down with a smile and accelerated abruptly, but he had to brake almost immediately, because he was about to bump the Simca; he blew the horn, and the boy looked at him in the rear-view mirror and made a gesture of helplessness, pointing to the Beaulieu, which was up against him. The Dauphine was three yards ahead, level with the Simca, and the little girl in the 203, now alongside the 404, waved her arms and showed him her doll. A red blot on his right confused 404; instead of the nuns' 2CV or the soldier's Volkswagen, he saw an unknown Chevrolet, and almost immediately the Chevrolet moved ahead followed by a Lancia and a Renault 8. To his left, an ID was gaining on him yard by yard, but before its place was taken by a 403, 404 was still able to make out up ahead the 203 that was already blocking Dauphine. The group was falling apart; it didn't exist anymore. Taunus had to be at least twenty yards away, followed by Dauphine; at the same time, the third row on the left was falling behind since, instead of the traveling salesman's DKW, 404 could see only the rear end of an old black van, perhaps a Citroën or a Peugeot. The cars were in third, gaining or losing ground according to the pace of their lane, and on the side of the thruway trees and some houses in the thick mist and dusk sped by. Later, it was the red lights they all turned on, following the example of those ahead, the night that suddenly closed in on them. From time to time, horns blew, speedometer needles climbed more and more, some lanes were going at forty-five miles an hour, others at forty, some at thirty-five. 404 still hoped that with the gaining and losing of ground he would again catch up with Dauphine, but each minute that slipped by convinced him that it was useless, that the group had dissolved irrevocably, that the everyday meetings would never take place again, the few rituals, the war councils in Taunus' car, Dauphine's caresses in the quiet of night, the children's laughter as they played with their little cars, the nun's face as she said her rosary. When the Simca's brake lights came on, 404 slowed down with an absurd feeling of hope, and as soon as he put on the handbrake he bolted out and ran ahead. Outside of the Simca and the Beaulieu (the Caravelle would be behind him, but he didn't care), he didn't recognize any cars; through strange windows faces he'd never seen before stared at him in surprise and perhaps even outrage. Horns began to blare, and 404 had to go back to his car; the boy in the Simca made a friendly gesture, pointing with encouragement toward Paris. The line got moving again, slowly for a few minutes, and later as if the thruway were completely free. On 404's left was a Taunus, and for a second 404 had the impression that the group was coming together again, that everything was returning to order, that it would be possible to move ahead without destroying anything. But it was a green Taunus, and there was a woman with dark glasses at the wheel who looked straight ahead. There was nothing to do but give in to the pace, adapt mechanically to the speed of the cars around, and not think. His leather jacket must still be in the soldier's Volkswagen. Taunus had the novel he had been reading the first few days. An almost empty bottle of lavender water was in the nuns' 2CV. And he had, there where he touched it at times with his right hand, the teddy bear Dauphine had given him as a pet. He clung absurdly to the idea that at nine-thirty the food would be distributed and the sick would have to be visited, the situation would have to be examined with Taunus and the farmer in the Ariane; then it would be night, Dauphine sneaking into his car, stars or clouds, life. Yes, it had to be like that. All that couldn't have ended forever. Maybe the soldier would get some water, which had been scarce the last few hours; at any rate, you could always count on Porsche, as long as you paid his price. And on the car's antenna the red-cross flag waved madly, and you moved at fifty-five miles an hour toward the lights that kept growing, not knowing why all this hurry, why this mad race in the night among unknown cars, where no one knew anything about the others, where everyone looked straight ahead, only ahead.

THE HEALTH OF THE SICK

When Aunt Clelia unexpectedly felt ill, there was a moment of panic in the family, and for several hours no one seemed able to face the situation and discuss a plan of action, not even Uncle Roque, who was always finding the most sensible way out. They called Carlos on the phone at the office, Rosa and Pepa dismissed their piano pupils, and even Aunt Clelia was more worried about Mama than about herself. She was sure that what she felt wasn't serious, but you couldn't give Mama upsetting news with her blood pressure and sugar content. They all very well knew that Doctor Bonifaz had been the first to understand and to approve their hiding from Mama what had happened to Alejandro. If Aunt Clelia had to be confined to bed, they would have to figure out something so that Mama wouldn't suspect she was sick, but already what had happened to Alejandro had become so difficult, and now this to boot; the slightest mistake, and she would find out the truth. The house was big, but you still had to keep in mind Mama's keen ear and her disturbing capacity for guessing where everyone was. Pepa, who had called Doctor Bonifaz from the upstairs telephone, warned her brother and sister that the doctor would come right away and that they should leave the front door ajar so he could enter without ringing. While Rosa and Uncle Roque attended to Aunt Clelia, who had fainted twice and was complaining of an unbearable headache, Carlos stayed with Mama to tell her about the new developments in the diplomatic conflict with Brazil and to read her the latest news. Mama was in a good mood that afternoon, and her back didn't hurt as it almost always did at siesta time. She asked each one of them what was the matter, they seemed so nervous, and everyone seemed to be talking about low air pressure and the horrid effects of additives in bread. At teatime, Uncle Roque came to chat with Mama so that Carlos could take a bath and wait downstairs for the doctor. Aunt Clelia was feeling better now, but it was an effort for her to move around in bed and she had almost no interest in what had worried her so much when she came out of the first dizzy spell. Pepa and Rosa took turns by her side, offering her tea and water without getting an answer; the house calmed down at dusk, and the brother and sisters thought that perhaps Aunt Clelia's wasn't serious and that the next afternoon she would again go into Mama's room as if nothing had happened.

With Alejandro, things had been worse, because Alejandro had been killed in a car accident shortly after reaching Montevideo, where he was expected at the house of an engineer friend. Already almost a year had passed since then, but it was always the first day for the family, for all except Mama. For Mama, Alejandro was in Brazil, where a Recife business firm had commissioned him to set up a cement factory. The idea of preparing Mama, of hinting to her that

Alejandro had had an accident and was slightly wounded, had not occurred to them, even after Doctor Bonifaz's warnings. Even María Laura, beyond all understanding in those first hours, had admitted that it was impossible to break the news to Mama. Carlos and María Laura's father went to Uruguay to bring back Alejandro's body, while the family, as usual, took care of Mama, who was distressed and difficult that day. The engineering club agreed to have the wake at its headquarters, and Pepa, the one most occupied with Mama, didn't even get to see Alejandro's coffin, while the others took turns every hour and accompanied the poor María Laura, lost in a tearless horror. As almost always, it was up to Uncle Roque to do the thinking. Early in the morning, he spoke to Carlos, who was crying silently for his brother with his head on the green cover of the dining room table, where they had so often played cards. Then Aunt Clelia joined them, because Mama slept the whole night, and they didn't have to worry about her. With Rosa's and Pepa's tacit agreement, they decided the first measures, beginning with the abduction of *La Nación*—at times, Mama got up the strength to read the newspaper for a few minutes—and all agreed with what Uncle Roque had thought up. It was that a Brazilian company had given Alejandro a contract to spend a year in Recife, and in a matter of hours Alejandro had to give up his brief vacation at the house of an engineer friend, pack his suitcase, and jump on the first plane. Mama had to understand that these were new times, that industrialists didn't know from sentiments, but that Alejandro would soon find a way to take a week's vacation in the middle of the year and come down to Buenos Aires. All this seemed very well to Mama, although she cried a little, and they had to bring her smelling salts. Carlos, who knew how to make her laugh, told her it was shameful to cry about their kid brother's first success and that Alejandro wouldn't like it if he knew they acted that way when they received the news of his contract. Then Mama calmed down and said that she would drink a bit of sherry to Alejandro's health. Carlos abruptly went out to get the wine, but it was Rosa who brought it and who toasted with Mama.

Mama's life was difficult, and although she seldom complained, they had to keep her company and distract her as much as possible. When, the day after Alejandro's funeral, she wondered why María Laura had not come to visit her as on every Thursday, Pepa went to the Novallis' house in the afternoon to speak to María Laura. At that hour, Uncle Roque was in a lawyer friend's study, explaining the situation to him; the lawyer promised to write immediately to his brother, who was working in Recife (cities were not chosen by chance in Mama's house), and organize the letter end. Doctor Bonifaz had already visited Mama as if by chance, and, after examining her sight, he found her considerably improved, but asked her to abstain from reading newspapers for a few days. Aunt Clelia was in charge of summarizing the most interesting news for her; luckily, Mama didn't like the radio newscasts, because they were common and every few minutes there were commercials on dubious medicines that people took come what may, and that's how they went.

María Laura came Friday afternoon and talked about all that she had to study for the architecture exams.

"Yes, my dear", Mama said, looking at her affectionately. "Your eyes are red from reading, and that's bad. Put some boric acid compresses on them—that's the best there is."

Rosa and Pepa were constantly there to assist during the conversation, and María Laura managed to endure it and even smiled when Mama started to go on about that naughty fiancé who went so far away and almost without warning. That was today's youth for you, the world had gone crazy, and everybody was in a hurry and had no time for anything. Then Mama lost the thread in the already well-known anecdotes about parents and grandparents, and the coffee came, and then Carlos came in with jokes and stories, and at one point Uncle Roque stood in the door of the bedroom and looked at them in his good-natured way, and everything went as it always did until it was time for Mama's rest.

The family got used to it; it was harder for María Laura, but then again she had to see Mama only on Thursdays. One day, Alejandro's first letter arrived (Mama had already wondered twice about his silence), and Carlos read it at the foot of the bed. Alejandro was delighted with Recife, he talked about the port and the parrot-sellers and the delicious cold drinks. Everybody's mouth watered in the family when they found out that pineapples didn't cost a thing and that the coffee there was the real McCoy and had a fragrance . . . Mama asked them to show her the envelope and told them to give the stamp to the Marolda boy, who was a stamp collector, although she didn't approve of boys playing around with stamps, because afterwards they didn't wash their hands, and the stamps had been all over the place.

"They lick them to glue them on," Mama would always say, "and the germs stay on their tongue and incubate—it's a well-known fact. But give it to him anyway, he has so many already that one more . . ."

The next day Mama called Rosa in and dictated a letter for Alejandro, asking him when he'd be able to take a vacation and if the trip wouldn't cost too much. She explained how she felt and spoke of the promotion they had just given Carlos and of the prize that one of Pepa's pupils had won. She also told him that María Laura visited her every Thursday without fail, but that she studied too much, and that was bad for the eyes. When the letter was written, Mama signed it at the bottom in pencil and gently kissed the paper. Pepa got up with the pretext of going for an envelope, and Aunt Clelia came in with the five o'clock pills and some flowers for the vase on the bureau.

It was not easy, because during that time Mama's blood pressure went up even more, and the family got to wondering if there wasn't some unconscious influence, something that showed from their behavior, an anxiety and depression that did Mama harm, despite the precautions and false gaiety. But it couldn't be, because just by pretending to laugh they all had ended up by really laughing with Mama, and at times they made jokes and cuffed each other even when they weren't with her and then looked at each other as if suddenly waking up, and Pepa got very red, and Carlos lit a cigarette with his head slouched. The only thing that mattered though was that time pass and that Mama not realize anything. Uncle Roque had spoken with Doctor Bonifaz, and everybody agreed that they had to continue the merciful comedy, as Aunt Clelia called it, indefinitely. The only problem was María Laura's visits, because Mama naturally insisted upon talking about Alejandro. She wanted to know if they would get married as soon as he came back from Recife or if that crazy son of hers was going to accept another contract somewhere faraway and for such a long time again. The only thing to do was to constantly go into the bedroom and distract Mama and remove María Laura, who would keep very still in her chair, squeezing her hands so tight that she'd hurt herself, but one day, Mama asked Aunt Clelia why everybody rushed in like that when María Laura came to see her, as if it were the only opportunity they had to be with her. Aunt Clelia laughed and said that they all saw a little of Alejandro in María Laura, and that's why they liked to be with her when she came.

"You're right. María Laura is so good," Mama said. "That rascally son of mine doesn't deserve her, believe you me."

"Look who's talking," Aunt Clelia said. "Why, you drool every time you mention your son."

Mama also laughed and remembered that they would be getting a letter from Alejandro any day then. The letter came, and Uncle Roque brought it with the five o'clock tea. This time, Mama wanted to read the letter and asked for her reading glasses. She read industriously, as if each sentence were a tasty morsel that she had to savor slowly.

"The boys today don't have respect," she said, without giving it too much importance. "All right, so in my time they didn't use those machines, but still I would never have dared write to my father that way, and you neither."

"Of course not," Uncle Roque said. "With the temper the old man had."

"When will you stop saying 'the old man,' Roque. You know I don't like to hear you say that, but you don't care. Remember how Mama would get."

"O.K., take it easy. 'The old man' is just a manner of speaking, it has nothing to do with respect."

"It's very strange," Mama said, taking off her glasses and looking at the moldings on the ceiling. "We've already gotten five or six letters from Alejandro, and in none of them has he called me . . . Oh, it's a secret between the two of us. It's strange, you know. Why hasn't he called me that, not even once?"

"Maybe the boy thinks it's silly to put it on paper. Saying is one thing . . . what is it he says? . . ."

"It's a secret," Mama said. "A secret between my little son and myself."

Neither Pepa nor Rosa knew what it was, and Carlos shrugged his shoulders when they asked him.

"What more do you want, Uncle? The most I can do is forge his signature. Mama will forget about it in time, don't take it so much to heart."

Four or five months later, after a letter from Alejandro in which he explained how much he had to do (although he was happy because it was a great opportunity for a young engineer), Mama insisted it was time he took a vacation and came down to Buenos Aires. It seemed to Rosa, who was writing Mama's answer, that she was dictating more slowly, as if she had been thinking each sentence out.

"Who knows if the poor thing will be able to come?" Rosa commented, trying to sound offhand. "It would be a shame for him to make a wrong move precisely when it's going so well for him and he's so happy."

Mama continued the dictation as if she hadn't heard. Her health left much to be desired, and she would like to see Alejandro, even if it were only for a few days. Alejandro also had María Laura to think about—not that she thought he was neglecting his fiancée, but affection doesn't live on pretty words and promises alone. So, she hoped Alejandro would write soon with good news. Rosa noticed that Mama didn't kiss the paper after signing, but that she stared at the letter as if she wanted to record it in her memory. "Poor Alejandro," thought Rosa and then crossed herself quickly so that Mama wouldn't see.

"Look," Uncle Roque said to Carlos when they were alone that night for their domino game, "this is going to get serious. We've got to invent something plausible, or in the end she's going to realize."

"What can I say, Uncle? The best thing is for Alejandro to answer in a way that will keep her happy a while longer. The poor thing is in such delicate condition, you can't even think of . . ."

"Nobody said anything about that, boy. But I'm telling you, your mother is the kind that doesn't give up. I know, it runs in the family."

Mama read Alejandro's evasive letter without comment; he would try to get a vacation as soon as he handed in the plans for the first sector of the factory. When María Laura arrived that afternoon, Mama asked her to entreat Alejandro to come to Buenos Aires, even if for no more than a week. María Laura told Rosa afterwards that Mama had asked that of her at the only moment when no one else could hear her. Uncle Roque was the first to suggest what all of them had already thought so many times without daring to come out and say it, and when Mama dictated to Rosa another letter to Alejandro, insisting that he come, it was decided that the only thing left to do was to try and see if Mama was in good shape to receive the first disagreeable news. Carlos consulted Doctor Bonifaz, who prescribed prudence and a few drops. They let the necessary time pass, and one afternoon Uncle Roque came to sit at the foot of Mama's bed, while Rosa prepared maté and looked out the window of the balcony, beside the medicine chest.

"How do you like that? Now I'm starting to understand a little why this devil of a nephew can't make up his mind to come and see us," Uncle Roque said. "The thing is, he just didn't want to upset you, knowing that you're still not well."

Mama looked at him as if she didn't understand.

"The Novallis phoned today. It seems that María Laura received news from Alejandro. He's fine, but he won't be able to travel for a few months."

"Why won't he be able to travel?" Mama asked.

"Because there's something wrong with his foot, it

seems. The ankle, I think. We'll have to ask María Laura to find out what it is. Old man Novalli mentioned a fracture or something like that."

"Ankle fracture?" Mama said.

Before Uncle Roque could answer, Rosa was there with the bottle of salts. Doctor Bonifaz came immediately, and it was all over in a few hours, but they were long hours, and Doctor Bonifaz didn't leave the family until well into the night. Only two days later did Mama feel well enough to ask Pepa to write to Alejandro. When Pepa, who hadn't understood, came as always with the block and the pencil holder, Mama closed her eyes and refused with a nod.

"You write to him. Tell him to take good care of himself."

Pepa obeyed, not knowing why she was writing one sentence after another, since Mama wasn't going to read the letter. That night, she told Carlos that all the time she was writing at Mama's bedside, she was absolutely sure that Mama wasn't going to read or sign that letter. Her eyes remained closed, and she didn't open them until it was time for her medicinal tea; she seemed to have forgotten, to be thinking of other things.

Alejandro answered with the most natural tone in the world, explaining that he hadn't wanted to tell her about the fracture so as not to upset her. At first, they had made a mistake and put on a cast that had to be changed, but now he was better, and in a few weeks he'd be able to start walking again. Altogether he had some two months to go, although the worst part was that his work had been greatly delayed at the busiest moment, and . . .

Carlos, who read the letter out loud, had the impression that Mama wasn't listening to him like other times. From time to time, she looked at the clock, which in her was a sign of impatience. At seven, Rosa had to bring her the broth with Doctor Bonifaz's drops, and it was five after seven.

"Well", Carlos said, folding the letter. "Now you see that everything's O.K. Nothing's seriously wrong with the kid."

"Of course," Mama said. "Look, tell Rosa to hurry, will you?"

Mama listened attentively while María Laura told her all about Alejandro's fracture and even advised her to recommend some ankle rubs, which had done his father so much good the time he fell off a horse in Matanzas. Almost immediately, as if it were part of the same sentence, she asked if they couldn't give her some orange blossom water, which always cleared her head.

The first to speak was María Laura, that very afternoon. She said it to Rosa in the drawing room, before going, and Rosa stood there looking at her as if she couldn't believe her ears.

"Please," Rosa said, "how can you imagine such a thing?"

"I'm not imagining it, it's the truth," María Laura said. "And I'm not going there any more, Rosa. Ask me all you want, but I'm not going back to that room again."

When you get right down to it, María Laura's notion didn't seem that ridiculous, but Aunt Clelia summed up everyone's sentiment when she said that in a home like theirs a duty was a duty. It was Rosa's turn to go to the Novallis', but María Laura had such a fit of hysterics that they would just have to respect her decision; that same afternoon, Pepa and Rosa began to comment on how much the poor girl had to study and how tired she was. Mama didn't say anything, and when Thursday came along she didn't ask for María Laura. That Thursday marked ten months since Alejandro left for Brazil. The company was so satisfied with his services, that some weeks later they proposed a renewal of his contract for another year, providing he go to Belén immediately to install another factory. Uncle Roque thought this was just wonderful, a great triumph for a boy so young.

"Alejandro was always the smartest one," Mama said. "Just as Carlos is the most tenacious."

"You're right," Uncle Roque said, wondering what could have gotten into María Laura that day. "The truth is you've turned out some wonderful children, sister."

"Oh yes, I can't complain. Their father would have liked to have seen them grown up. The girls, so good, and poor Carlos, such a homebody."

"And Alejandro, with so much future ahead of him."

"Ah, yes," mama said.

"Why, that new contract alone that they're offering him . . . Oh well, you'll answer your son when you're in the mood, I suppose; he must be going around with his tail between his legs thinking the news of the renewal isn't going to please you."

"Ah, yes," Mama said again, looking at the ceiling. "Tell Pepa to write to him, she knows."

Pepa wrote, without being very sure of what she should say to Alejandro, but convinced that it was always better to have a complete text to avoid contradictions in the answers. As for Alejandro, he was very happy that Mama appreciated what an opportunity they were offering him. The ankle was doing fine, and he would ask for a vacation as soon as he could, to come and spend two weeks with them. Mama assented with a slight nod and asked if *La Razón* had arrived yet, so that Carlos could read her the cable news. Everything began to run smoothly in the house, now that there seemed to be no more surprises in store, and Mama's health remained stationary. Her children took turns at keeping her company; Uncle Roque and Aunt Clelia were constantly going in and out. Carlos read Mama the newspaper at night, and Pepa in the morning. Rosa and Aunt Clelia took care of the medications and baths; Uncle Roque had maté in her room two or three times a day. Mama was never alone and never asked for María Laura; every three weeks she received news of Alejandro without comment; she'd tell Pepa to answer and talk about something else, always intelligent and attentive and distant.

It was around then that Uncle Roque began to read her the news about tensions with Brazil. He had written the first reports on the edges of the newspapers, but Mama didn't care about the perfection of the reading, so after a few days Uncle Roque got used to improvising. At first, he accompanied the disturbing cablegrams with some comment on the problems this situation could cause Alejandro and the other Argentines in Brazil, but as Mama didn't seem to worry, he stopped insisting, although every few days the situation grew a little worse. In Alejandro's letter, the possibility of a break in diplomatic relations was mentioned, although the boy was as optimistic as ever and convinced that the chancellors would mend the dispute.

Mama would make no comments, perhaps because it was still a long time before Alejandro could request leave, but one night she suddenly asked Doctor Bonifaz if the situation with Brazil was as bad as the newspapers said.

"Brazil? Well, yes, things aren't going too well," the doctor said. "Let's hope that the statesmen have the good sense . . ."

Mama looked at him as if surprised that he had answered without hesitating. She sighed softly and changed the subject. That night, she was in better spirits than usual, and Doctor Bonifaz left satisfied. The next day, Aunt Clelia fell ill; the fainting spells seemed like a passing thing, but

Doctor Bonifaz spoke to Uncle Roque and advised them to put Aunt Clelia in a hospital. They told Mama, who was at that moment listening to the news about Brazil which Carlos brought with the evening paper, that Aunt Clelia was in bed with a migraine. They had the whole night to think about what they would do, but Uncle Roque was rather crushed after speaking to Doctor Bonifaz, and it was up to Carlos and the girls to decide. Rosa thought of Manolita Valle's villa and the good country air; the second day of Aunt Clelia's migraine, Carlos lead the conversation so well that it was as if Mama herself had advised a spell in Manolita's villa, which would do Clelia so much good. An office companion of Carlos' offered to take her in his car, since the train would be tiring with that migraine. Aunt Clelia was the first to want to say goodbye to Mama, and between them, Carlos and Uncle Roque led her step by step, so that Mama could tell her not to catch cold in those automobiles they have today and to remember to take her fruit laxative at night.

"Clelia looked red in the face," Mama said to Pepa that afternoon. "She looked bad to me, you know."

"Oh, after a few days in the country she'll be fine again. She's been a bit tired these last few months; I remember Manolita telling her she should come keep her company at the villa."

"Really? That's strange, she never told me."

"So as not to upset you, I suppose."

"And how long is she going to stay, dear?"

Pepa didn't know, but she would ask Doctor Bonifaz, who was the one who had advised the change of air. Mama didn't speak of the matter again until some days later. (Aunt Clelia had just had a stroke in the hospital, and Rosa took turns at keeping her company with Uncle Roque.)

"I wonder when Clelia's coming back," Mama said.

"Come on, the one time the poor thing makes up her mind to leave you and get a change of air . . ."

"Yes, but what she had was nothing, you all said."

"Of course it's nothing. She must be staying on because she likes it, or to keep Manolita company; you know what good friends they are."

"Phone the villa and find out when she's coming back," Mama said.

Rosa phoned the villa, and they told her that Aunt Clelia was better, but that she still felt a bit weak, so that she would take the opportunity to stay. The weather was splendid in Olavarría.

"I don't like that at all," Mama said. "Clelia should have come home by now."

"Please, Mama, don't worry so much. Why don't you get better as soon as you can and go sunbathe with Clelia and Manolita at the villa?"

"Me?" mama said, looking at Carlos as if astonished, outraged, insulted. Carlos laughed to hide what he felt (Aunt Clelia was in critical condition, Pepa had just phoned) and kissed her on the cheek as if she were a naughty child.

"Silly little Mama," he said, trying not to think of anything.

That night, Mama slept badly and at daybreak asked for Clelia, as if they could have heard from the villa at that hour. (Aunt Clelia had just died, and they had decided to have her wake at the funeral home.) At eight o'clock, they called the villa from the living room telephone, so that Mama could listen to the conversation, and luckily Aunt Clelia had had a good night, although Manolita's doctor advised her to stay while the good weather continued. Carlos was very happy, since the office was closed for the annual financial statement, and he came in, in pajamas, to have his maté at the foot of Mama's bed and chat with her.

"Look," Mama said, "I think we should write to Alejandro and tell him to come see his aunt. He was always Clelia's favorite, and it's only right that he should come."

"But Aunt Clelia doesn't have anything, Mama. If Alejandro hasn't been able to come and see you, imagine . . ."

"That's up to him," Mama said. "You write and tell him that Clelia is sick and that he should come see her."

"But how many times do we have to tell you that what Aunt Clelia has isn't serious?"

"All the better. But it won't do any harm to write him."

They wrote that same afternoon and read the letter to Mama. During the days when Alejandro's letter would be arriving (Aunt Clelia was still doing fine, but Manolita's doctor insisted that she take advantage of the good country air), the diplomatic situation with Brazil got even worse, and Carlos told Mama that it wouldn't be surprising if Alejandro's letters were delayed.

"It would almost seem on purpose," Mama said. "Now you'll see that he won't be able to come either."

None of them could make up his mind to read her Alejandro's letter.

All together at the dining room table, they looked at Aunt Clelia's empty place, then looked at each other, hesitating.

"This is ridiculous. We're so used to this comedy already, that one scene more or less . . ."

"Then you take it to her" Pepa said, while her eyes filled with tears and she dried them with her napkin.

"Whatever you do, there's something wrong somehow. Each time I go into her room now it feels like I'm expecting a surprise, a trap, almost."

"It's María Laura's fault," Rosa said. She put the idea

into our heads, and we can't act naturally anymore. And to top it off, Aunt Clelia . . ."

"Well, now that you mention it, I think it would be a good idea to talk to María Laura," Uncle Roque said. "It would be the most logical thing for her to come visit after her exams and bring your mother the news that Alejandro won't be able to come."

"But doesn't it make your blood run cold that Mama doesn't ask for María Laura anymore, even though Alejandro mentions her in all his letters?"

"The temperature of my blood has nothing to do with it," Uncle Roque said. "You either do it or don't do it, and that's that."

It took Rosa two hours to convince María Laura, but she was her best friend, and María Laura loved them all dearly, even Mama, although she had frightened her. They had to prepare a new letter, which María Laura brought along with a bouquet of flowers and the mandarine orange drops that mama liked. Yes, luckily the worst exams were over, and she could go to San Vicente for a few weeks to rest.

"The country air will do you good," Mama said. "Now with Clelia . . . Did you call the villa today, Pepa? Oh yes, I remember that you told me . . . Well, it's been three weeks since Clelia left, and just look . . ."

María Laura and Rosa made the obvious comments, the tea tray came, and María Laura read Mama some paragraphs from Alejandro's letter with the news of the temporary imprisonment of all foreign technicians, and how funny he thought it was to be living in a splendid hotel at the government's expense, while waiting for the chancellors to mend the dispute. Mama made no comment, drank her cup of linden flower tea and became sleepy. The girls continued their conversation in the living room, relieved. María Laura was about to go, when she suddenly thought of the telephone and told Rosa. It seemed to Rosa that Carlos, too, had thought of that, and later she spoke to Uncle Roque, who shrugged his shoulders. Faced with something like that, the only thing you could do was to keep reading the newspaper. But Rosa and Pepa also told Carlos about it, who refused to look for a solution except that of accepting what nobody wanted to accept.

"We'll see," Carlos said. "She still may think of that and ask for it. In which case . . ."

But Mama never asked them to bring her the telephone so that she could speak personally with Aunt Clelia. Every morning she asked if there was news from the villa and then returned to her silence, where time seemed to be measured in doses of medicine and medicinal tea. She wasn't displeased when Uncle Roque came with *La Razón* to read the latest news about the conflict with Brazil, but neither did she seem to care if the newsboy was late or if Uncle Roque was more occupied than usual with a chess problem. Rosa and Pepa became convinced that Mama didn't care if they read her the news, or phoned the villa, or brought a letter from Alejandro. But you couldn't be sure, because sometimes Mama raised her head and looked at them with that same profound look, in which there was no change, no acceptance. Routine took over, and for Rosa, phoning a black hole at the end of the line was as simple and everyday as reading false cable news on a background of sales advertisements or soccer news was for Uncle Roque, or as coming in with stories of his visit to the Olavarría villa and of the baskets of fruit Manolita and Aunt Clelia sent them was for Carlos. Not even during Mama's last months did they change their habits, although they had little importance by then. Doctor Bonifaz told them that, fortunately, Mama would not suffer at all and that she would pass away without feeling it. But Mama remained clear-headed until the end, when her children came around her, unable to hide what they felt.

"How good you were to me," Mama said. "All that trouble you went through so I wouldn't suffer."

Uncle Roque was sitting beside her and he caressed her hand cheerfully, saying how silly she was. Pepa and Rosa, pretending to look for something in the bureau, now knew that María Laura had been right; they knew what in some way they had always known.

"Such good care of me . . . ," Mama said, and Pepa squeezed Rosa's hand, because, after all, those five words put everything back into order, reestablished the long and necessary comedy. But Carlos, at the foot of the bed, looked at Mama as if he knew she was going to say something further.

"Now you'll all be able to relax," Mama said. "We won't give you any more trouble."

Uncle Roque was going to protest, to say something, but Carlos went to him and violently squeezed his shoulder. Mama was slipping gradually into a doze, and it was better not to bother her.

Three days after the funeral, Alejandro's last letter arrived, in which, as always, he asked about Mama's and Aunt Clelia's health. Rosa opened it and began reading without a second thought, and when she raised her eyes because they were suddenly blinded with tears, she realized that while she was reading, she had been thinking about how she was going to break the news to Alejandro that Mama was dead.

M E E T I N G

I recalled a Jack London story in which
the hero [. . .] leans calmly against a tree
and prepares to die in a dignified manner.
——*Ernesto "Che" Guevara, in* Episodes of
the Revolutionary War, *1968 (originally
from* La sierra y el llano, *Havana, 1961).*

THINGS COULDN'T BE WORSE, but at least we were no longer
in the damn yacht, rolling in vomit and high seas and wet
crackers and machine guns and drivel, filthy dirty, soothing
ourselves when we could with the little tobacco that remained dry because Luis (whose name wasn't Luis, but we
had sworn not to remember our names until that day arrived) had had the good sense to put it into a tin box that
we would open more carefully than if it had been full of
scorpions. But not even tobacco or slugs of rum in that
goddamn yacht, swaying five days like a drunken turtle,
facing a northerly wind that whipped it mercilessly, waves
coming and going, the buckets scraping the skin off our
hands, me with an infernal asthma attack and almost everybody seasick, doubling over to vomit as if they were going
to split in half. Even Luis, the second night, a green bile that
dampened his spirits, between that and the northerly that
kept us from seeing the Cabo Cruz Light, a disaster which

nobody had expected; and to call that a landing expedition was enough to keep you vomiting but out of pure sadness. Oh well, anything to be able to leave the yacht behind, anything, even though it would be what was waiting for us on land—but we knew what was waiting for us and that's why it didn't matter so much—the weather that clears up at precisely the wrong time and wham the reconnaissance plane, what can you do, ford the swamp or whatever it is, with the water up to your ribs, seeking the cover of the dirty grasslands and mangroves, and me like an idiot with my adrenalin spray to keep me going, with Roberto carrying my Springfield to help me make it through the swamp (if it was a swamp, because the thought had already occurred to many of us that we might have gone off course and that instead of land we had blundered into some muddy shoal in the sea, twenty miles from the island . . .); and everything the same, badly planned and hopelessly executed, in a continuous confusion of acts and notions, a mixture of inexplicable joy and of anger at the hard time the planes were giving us and at what was waiting for us on the highway if we ever got there, if we were in a swamp on the coast and not going around in circles like duped clowns in a circus of mud and of total failure for the amusement of the baboon in his Palace.

Now nobody remembers how long it lasted, we measured the time by the clearings in the grasslands, the pieces of land where they could gun us down in a dive, the scream I heard on my left, faraway, and that I think was Roque's (I can give him, his poor skeleton among the lianas and toads, his own name). Because of all the plans, only the final goal remained, to reach the Sierra and meet up with Luis if he also managed to get there; the rest had been torn to shreds by the northerly, the makeshift landing, the marshes. But let's be fair: Something did happen on schedule, the

attack of the enemy planes. It had been expected and pro-
voked; it didn't fail. And that's why, even though Roque's
cry still made my face ache, my malignant way of understanding the world helped me to laugh, cautiously (and I
choked even more, and Roberto carried the Springfield so
that I could inhale adrenalin with my nose almost in the
water, swallowing more mud than anything else), because if
the planes were there it meant we couldn't have gotten the
wrong beach, we had gone off a few miles at the most, but
the highway would be beyond the grasslands, and then the
open field and to the north the first hills. The fact that the
enemy affirmed the excellence of our landing had its comic
side.

It lasted God knows how long, and afterwards it was
night, and there were six of us under some thin trees, for the
first time on almost dry land, chewing damp tobacco and
some miserable crackers. From Luis, Pablo, Lucas, no news;
scattered, probably dead, in any case as lost and wet as we
were. But I liked feeling how, with the end of that am-
phibian march, my ideas began to organize, and how death,
more probable than ever, would no longer be a chance bullet
in the middle of a swamp but a dryly dialectic operation,
perfectly orchestrated by the parts in play. The army must
have been controlling the highway, surrounding the marshes, waiting for us to come out in twos and threes, exhausted by the mud and varmints and hunger. Now I could
see it all clearly, again I had the cardinal points in my pocket,
it made me laugh to feel so alive and so awake on the verge
of the epilogue. Nothing seemed funnier to me than to get
Roberto mad by reciting some of old Pancho's verses in his
ear, which he found abominable. "If only we could get rid
of the mud," the Lieutenant complained. "Or smoke for
real" (someone, more to the left, I no longer know who,

someone we lost at dawn). Organization of the death agony:
sentries, sleeping by turns, chewing tobacco, sucking crackers swollen like sponges. Nobody mentioned Luis, the fear
that they had killed him was the only real enemy, because
its confirmation would nullify us more than the pursuit, the
lack of weapons, or our blistered feet. I know that I slept
while Roberto kept watch, but before that, I was thinking
that all we had done in those days was too reckless for us to
suddenly admit the possibility that they had killed Luis. In
some way, the recklessness would have to continue until the
end, which would perhaps be victory, and in that absurd
game which had reached the scandalous proportions of letting the enemy know that we were landing, the possibility
of losing Luis did not enter. I believe I also thought that if
we triumphed, if we managed to meet up again with Luis,
only then would the game really begin, the atonement for
so much necessary and unbridled and dangerous romanti-
cism. Before falling asleep I had a sort of vision: Luis beside
a tree, surrounded by all of us, slowly raised his hand to his
face and took it off as if it were a mask. With his face in
his hand he approached his brother Pablo, myself, the Lieutenant, Roque, asking us with a gesture to accept it, to put
it on. But they all refused one by one, and I also refused,
smiling myself to tears, and then Luis put his face on again
and I saw in him an infinite weariness as he shrugged his
shoulders and took a cigarette out of the pocket of his shirt.
Professionally speaking, a hallucination from light sleep and
fever, easily interpreted. But if they had really killed Luis
during the landing, who would go up to the Sierra now with
his face? We would all try to get up there, but none with
Luis' face. "The Diadochi," I thought, already half-asleep.
"But it all went to pot with the Diadochi, everybody knows
that."

· · ·

Although this story happened a while back, pieces and moments remain so clearly etched in my memory that they can be told only in present tense, like being flat on our backs again in the grass, beside the tree that shelters us from the open sky. It's the third night, but at the dawn of that day we crossed the highway in spite of the jeeps and the machine guns. Now we've got to wait for another dawn because they've killed our guide and we're lost, we'll have to find some peasant who can take us to where we can buy something to eat, and when I say buy it almost makes me laugh and I choke again, but in that as in the rest nobody would think of disobeying Luis, and we've got to pay for the food and explain to the people who we are and why we're doing what we're doing. Roberto's expression in the abandoned hut on the hill, leaving five pesos under a plate in exchange for the little we found and which tasted like heaven, like the food in the Ritz if people really do eat well there. I have so much fever my asthma is going away, well, every cloud has its silver lining, but again I think of Roberto's expression leaving the five pesos in the empty hut, and it makes me laugh so hard that I choke again and curse myself. We should sleep now, Tinti stands guard, the boys rest against each other, I have gone a little further away because I have the impression that I bother them with my cough and wheeze, and besides I do something that I shouldn't, which is that two or three times a night I make a screen of leaves and put my face underneath and slowly light the cigar to reconcile myself with life a little.

In substance the only good thing all day has been not getting any news about Luis, the rest is a disaster, out of eighty they've killed fifty or sixty of us; Javier was among the first to fall, the Peruvian lost an eye and lay dying for three hours without my being able to do anything, not even finish him off when the others weren't looking. The whole day we feared that some runner (three had gotten through with incredible risk, under the very noses of the enemy) would bring us the news of Luis' death. In the end it's better to know nothing, to imagine him alive, to be able to keep waiting. Coldly I weigh the possibilities and conclude that they've killed him, we all know how he is, how the damn fool is capable of going out into the open with a pistol in his hand, and the devil may care. No, López must have taken care of him, nobody can fool him the way he does sometimes, almost treating him like a kid, convincing him that he has to do the opposite of what he feels like doing in that moment. But, if López . . . No use worrying myself to death, we have no basis for any conjecture, and besides this calm is strange, this easy life flat on our backs as if everything were just fine, as if our mission had been accomplished (I almost thought: "had been consummated," which would have been stupid) as planned. It could be the fever or the fatigue, it could be the fact that they're going to exterminate us all like toads before the sun comes out. But now it's worth taking advantage of this absurd moment of rest, letting myself look at the sketch of the tree branches against the clearer sky, with some stars, following with half-closed eyes that casual design of the branches and leaves, those rhythms that meet, ride upon each other, and separate, and sometimes gently change when a whiff of boiling air passes over the treetops, coming from the swamps. I think of my son but he's far away, thousands of miles away, in a country where they still sleep in bed, and his image seems unreal to me, it tapers, and disappears among the leaves of the tree, and instead it does me so much good to remember a Mozart theme that has always been with me, the first movement of *The Hunt* quartet, the evocation of the *hallali*, the death flourish, in the gentle voice of the violins, that transposing of a savage rite to a clear introspective joy. I think it, I repeat it, I hum it in my memory, and at the same time feel how the melody and the sketch of the treetop against the sky draw near, become friends, feel each other out a few times until the sketch is suddenly organized into the visible presence of the melody, a rhythm coming from a lower branch, almost at the level of my head, rises to a certain height and then opens like a fan of stems, while the second violin is that thinner branch placing itself next to the other, to fuse its leaves into a point situated to the right, toward the end of the phrase, letting it end so that the eye moves down the trunk and can, if it wishes, repeat the melody. And all that is also our rebellion, it is what we are doing, even though Mozart and the tree cannot know, we, too, in our way, have wanted to transpose a clumsy war into an order that gives it meaning, justifies it, and finally carries it to a victory that might be like the restoration of a melody after so many years of raucous hunting horns, it might be that final allegro which follows the adagio like an encounter with light. What a kick Luis would get out of knowing that in this moment I am comparing him to Mozart, seeing him put this recklessness to order little by little, raising it to its primal reason which annihilates with its evidence and its excess all prudent temporal reasons. But what a bitter, what a desperate task to be a musician of men, to plot, despite mud and bullets and discouragement, that song we believed impossible, the song that will make friends with the treetop, with the earth returned to its sons! Yes, it is fever. And how Luis would laugh, although he, too, likes Mozart, I am sure.

And so in the end I'll fall asleep, but before that I shall manage to wonder if some day we will know how to pass from the movement where the hunter's *hallali* still sounds, to the conquered fullness of the adagio and from there to the final allegro which I hum with a thread of voice, if we will be capable of reaching the reconciliation with all that has remained alive in front of us. We would have to be like Luis, no longer follow him but be like him, leave hate and vengeance irrepealably behind, look at the enemy as Luis looks at him, with a relentless magnanimity which has so often revived in my memory (but how can I say this to anyone?) an image of a Pantocrator, a judge who begins by being the accused and the witness and who does not judge, who simply separates the lands from the waters so that finally, someday, a nation of men is born on a trembling dawn, on the banks of a cleaner time.

But what an adagio! Why, with the first light, they were on us from all sides, and we had to forget about continuing northeast and head into a poorly known area, wasting the last ammunition while the Lieutenant along with a comrade held a hill and from there stopped them short for a while, giving Roberto and myself time to carry Tinti wounded in his thigh, and find another more sheltered spot higher up to hold up in until nightfall. They never attacked at night although they had flares and electrical equipment; a kind of terror of feeling less protected by numbers and their wasting of weapons would come over them; but until night we had almost a whole day to get through, and we were only five against those courageous boys who harassed us to be in good standing with the baboon, not counting the planes that dived into the clearings in the woods from time to time and spoiled a quantity of palm trees with their bursts of fire.

A half-hour later the Lieutenant ceased fire and joined us; we had made little headway. As nobody even thought of abandoning Tinti—we knew only too well the fate of prisoners—we figured that there, on that slope and in those thickets, we would burn the last cartridges. It was funny to learn that instead the regulars were attacking a hill quite off to the east, deceived by an aeronautical error, and so we headed uphill on a hellish path, reaching two hours later an almost bald hill where a comrade had the good eye to find a cave covered by tall grass, and we sat down breathing hard after calculating a possible retreat directly north, from rock to rock, dangerous but to the north, toward the Sierra where maybe Luis had already arrived.

While I tended unconscious Tinti, the Lieutenant told me that a little before the regulars' attack at daybreak he had heard the fire of automatic rifles and pistols toward the west. It could be Pablo with his boys, or maybe even Luis. We had the reasonable conviction that the survivors were divided into three groups, and perhaps Pablo's wasn't so far off. The Lieutenant asked me if wouldn't it be worth while sending a runner at nightfall.

"If you're asking me it's because you're offering to go," I told him. We had laid Tinti down on a bed of dry grass, in the coolest part of the cave, and we rested and smoked. The other comrades stood guard outside.

"Can you imagine that, kid?" the Lieutenant said to me, looking amused. "I get a kick out of these little excursions."

We went on like that for a while, joking with Tinti, who was getting delirious, and when the Lieutenant was about to go, in came Roberto with a mountaineer and a side of roast kid goat. We couldn't believe it, we ate like one who eats a ghost. Even Tinti nibbled on a piece which he would vomit two hours later along with his life. The mountaineer brought us news of Luis' death; we didn't stop eating for that, but it was a lot of salt for so little meat. He had not seen him, but his eldest son, who also had stuck to us with an old hunting rifle, formed part of the group that had helped Luis and five comrades ford a river under machine gun fire, and he was sure that Luis had been wounded almost before coming out of the water and before he could reach the first bushes. The mountaineers had climbed through the woods they knew better than anybody, and with them two men from Luis' group, who would arrive by night with more than enough weapons and some ammunition.

The Lieutenant lit another cigar and went out to organize the camp and get to know the new men better; I stayed beside Tinti, who was sinking slowly, almost painlessly. That is to say Luis had died, the kid goat was *finger-lickin'* good, that night there would be nine or ten of us, and we would have ammunition to continue fighting. Some news! It was like a kind of cold madness which on one hand reinforced the present with men and food, but all that to erase the future in one blow, the very reason for this recklessness which had just come to an end with a piece of news and a taste of roast kid goat. In the darkness of the cave, making my cigar last, I felt in that moment I could not allow myself the luxury of accepting Luis' death, I could handle it only as one more datum within the campaign plan, because if Pablo had died, too, I was the leader by Luis' will, and the Lieutenant and all the comrades knew that, and the only thing to do was to take command and reach the Sierra and keep going as if nothing had happened. I believe I closed my eyes, and the memory of my vision was again the vision itself, and for a second it seemed that Luis separated himself from his face and offered it to me, and I defended my face with my two hands saying: "No, no, please no, Luis," and when I opened my eyes the Lieutenant was back looking at Tinti, who was breathing heavily, and I heard him say that two boys from the woods had just joined us, nothing but good news, ammunition and fried sweet potatoes, a medicine chest, the regulars lost in the east hills, fabulous spring water fifty yards away. But he didn't look me in the eyes, he

chewed his cigar and seemed to wait for me to say something, for me to be the first to mention Luis again.

Afterwards there's a sort of confused gap, Tinti lost his
blood and we him, the mountaineers offered to bury him,
I remained resting in the cave although it smelled of vomit
and cold sweat, and curiously I got to thinking about my best
friend of former times, of before that break in my life that
had torn me from my country and thrust me thousands of
miles away, to Luis, to the landing on the island, to that
cave. Calculating the time difference I imagined that at that
moment, Wednesday, he would be walking into his office,
hanging his hat on the hook, glancing over the mail. It
wasn't an hallucination, it was enough just to think of those
years in which we had lived so close to one another in the
city, sharing politics, women, and books, meeting daily in
the hospital; every one of his gestures was so familiar to me,
and those gestures were not only his but embraced my whole
world then, myself, my wife, my father, my newspaper with
its inflated editorials, my midday coffee with the doctors on
duty, my readings and my movies and my ideals. I wondered
what my friend would be thinking about all that, of Luis or
of me, and it was as if I saw the answer written on his face
(but that was the fever, I would have to take quinine), a
self-satisfied face, filled out by the good life and good editions and the efficiency of the accredited surgeon's knife. It
wasn't even necessary for him to open his mouth to tell me
I think your revolution is nothing but . . . It wasn't necessary
but it had to be that way, those people could not accept a
change that uncovered the real reasons for their easy and
timetabled mercy, their regulated and metered charity, their
good nature among equals, their drawing room liberalism
but what do you mean our daughter's going to marry that
mulatto, huh, their Catholicism with its annual dividend
and ephemeris in the bannered squares, their tapioca litera-

ture, their folklore in numbered copies and maté with a silver sipper, their gatherings of genuflecting chancellors, their stupid inevitable short- or long-term death agony (quinine, quinine, and again asthma). I felt pity at imagining him defending like an idiot precisely the false values that would be the end of him or at best his sons; defending the feudal right to property and unlimited wealth, he who had only his doctor's office and a nice house, defending the principles of the Church when his wife's bourgeois Catholicism had served only to make him look for comfort in mistresses, defending a supposed individual freedom when the police closed the universities and censored publications, and defending out of fear, out of a horror of change, out of skepticism and mistrust which were the only living gods in his poor lost country. And that's what I was thinking when the Lieutenant rushed in shouting that Luis was alive, that they had just made a connection with the north, that Luis was more alive than a son of a bitch, he had reached the top of the Sierra with fifty peasants and all the weapons they had gotten off a battalion of regulars cornered in a ravine, and we hugged each other like idiots and said those things that afterwards, for a long time, bring you anger and shame and perfume, because that and eating roast goat and pushing on were the only things that made sense, that counted, and grew while we didn't dare look each other in the eye and lit cigars on the firebrand, with our eyes staring at the firebrand and drying the tears the smoke drew from us with its known tear-producing properties.

There's not much left to tell now. At daybreak one of our mountaineers took the Lieutenant and Roberto to where Pablo and his three comrades were, and the Lieutenant lifted Pablo in his arms because his feet were mangled from the swamps. Now we were twenty, I remember Pablo hugging me in his quick and expedient way, and saying to me without taking his cigarette out of his mouth: "If Luis is alive, we can still win," and I bandaging his feet, which was beautiful, and the boys pulling his leg because it looked like he was showing off new white shoes and telling him that his brother would scold him for that inappropriate luxury. "Let him scold me," Pablo joked smoking like crazy. "To scold someone you have to be alive, pal, and you've heard he's alive, haven't you, more alive than an alligator, and we're going up there right now, boy you've put some bandages on me, there's luxury for you . . ." But it couldn't last, with the sun came the lead from above and below, at some point a bullet grazed me on the ear that, had it been two inches more accurate, you, son, who may be reading all this, would be left without knowing what your old man was up to. With the blood and the pain and the fright, things went stereoscopic on me, each image clear-cut, in bas-relief, in colors that must have been my desire to live and besides there was nothing wrong with me, a handkerchief firmly tied and keep moving; but two mountaineers stayed behind, and Pablo's adjutant with a .45 bullet hole in his face. In those moments silly things get fixed forever in your mind; I remember a fat guy, from Pablo's group, too, I think, who in the worst of the battle tried to hide behind a stalk of sugar cane, kneeling in profile behind the cane, and I especially remember that someone began shouting that we had to surrender, and then a voice that answered him between two bursts of a Thompson gun, the Lieutenant's voice, a roar above the shooting, a: "No, fuck it, nobody surrenders here!" until the shortest of the mountaineers, so quiet and shy up until then, let me know that there was a path 100 yards from there, twisting upward and to the left, and I shouted it to the Lieutenant and I took the lead with the mountaineers following me and shooting like all hell broke loose, in the thick of a baptism of fire and savoring the pleasure of seeing them at it, and finally we all joined at the ceiba tree where the path began and the little mountaineer climbed with us behind him, me with an asthma that didn't even let me walk and the back of my neck more bloody than a pig with his head chopped off, but also sure that we would escape that day, I don't know why, but it was as evident as a theorem that that very night we would meet up with Luis.

You can never figure out how you leave your pursuers behind. Little by little the fire tapers off, then the familiar cursing and "Cowards, they split instead of fighting," then suddenly it's silence, the trees are again living and friendly things, the bumps in the terrain, the wounded that must be tended, the canteen of water with a little rum that runs from mouth to mouth, the sighs, someone complains, the moment of rest and the cigar, keep moving, climb climb although my lungs be coming out of my ears, and Pablo saying to me hey, you made them forty-two and my size is forty-three, pal, and the laughter, the top of the hill, the hut where a peasant had a little yuca with sauce and very cool water, and Roberto, persistent and finicky, taking out his four pesos to pay the expense and everybody, beginning with the peasant, laughing themselves sick, and midday inviting that siesta we had to refuse as if we were letting a pretty girl get away, looking at her legs till the last.

At nightfall the path got steeper and more difficult, but we licked our chops thinking of the position Luis had chosen to wait for us, not even a deerbuck could get up there. "It'll be like being in a church," Pablo said at my side, "we even have a harmonium," and he looked at me jokingly while I panted a kind of passacaglia which only he thought funny. I don't remember those hours very clearly, it was getting dark when we reached the first sentry and passed one after the other, letting them know who we were and answering for the mountaineers as well, until finally stepping into the clearing between the trees where Luis was leaning on a tree trunk, wearing, naturally, his cap with its perennial eyeshade and the cigar in his mouth. It was as hard as hell to stay behind, letting Pablo run and hug his brother, and then waiting for the Lieutenant and the others to also embrace him, and then I put the medicine chest and the Springfield down and with my hands in my pockets walked over and stood looking at him, knowing what he was going to say, the same old joke:

"Still using those silly eyeglasses," Luis said.

"And you those spectacles," I answered, and we doubled over with laughter, and his jaw against my face made my bullet hurt like hell, but it was a pain I would have liked to have felt forever.

"So you made it, Che," Luis said.

Naturally, he said "Che" very badly.

"What d'ya think?" I answered him, equally badly. And we doubled over like idiots, and almost everybody laughed without knowing why. They brought water and the news, we made the usual circle around Luis, and only then did we realize how thin he'd grown and how his eyes shined behind the damn spectacles.

Further below they were fighting again, but the camp was momentarily safe from danger. We could tend the wounded, bathe in the spring, sleep, above all sleep, even Pablo who wanted so much to speak to his brother. But as asthma is my mistress and has taught me to take advantage of the night, I sat with Luis against the trunk of a tree, smoking and looking at the sketches of the leaves against the sky and we talked from time to time about what had happened to us since the landing, but above all we talked about the future, about what was going to begin that day when

we'd have to move from the rifle to the office with tele-
phones, from the mountains to the city, and I remembered
the hunting horns and I was about to tell Luis what I had
thought that night, just to make him laugh. In the end I
didn't tell him, but I felt that we were passing into the
adagio of the quartet, into a precarious plenitude a few hours
old which nevertheless was a certainty, a sign that we
wouldn't forget. How many hunting horns still waited, how
many of us would leave our bones like Roque, like Tinti, like
the Peruvian. But it was enough to look at the treetop to feel
that the will again put its chaos to order, imposed on it the
sketch of the adagio that would some day pass into the final
allegro and accede to a reality worthy of that name. And
while Luis was bringing me up to date on international news
and on what was happening in the capital and provinces, I
saw how the leaves and branches were bending little by little
to my desire, they were my melody, Luis' melody whose talk
was miles apart from my fantasies, and then I saw a star
inscribed in the center of the sketch, and it was a little star
and very blue, and though I don't know anything about
astronomy and wouldn't be able to say whether it was a star
or a planet, I did feel sure that it was neither Mars nor
Mercury, it shined too much in the center of the adagio, too
much in the center of Luis' words to be mistaken for Mars
or Mercury.

Nurse Cora

*We'll send your love to college, all for a
year or two,
And then perhaps in time the boy will do
for you.*
——The trees that grow so high. (*English
folksong.*)

I CAN'T UNDERSTAND WHY they don't let me spend the night
in the hospital with the baby, after all I'm his mother and
Doctor de Luisi recommended us personally to the director.
They could bring a sofa bed and I could keep him company
until he gets used to it, the poor thing was so pale when he
came in as if they were going to operate right away, it must
be that hospital smell, his father was nervous, too, he
couldn't wait to leave, but I was sure they'd let me stay with
the baby. After all he's only fifteen and you'd never know
it, sticking to me all the time although with his long pants
now he wants to fool people and play the grownup. How he
must have felt when he realized they wouldn't let me stay,
a good thing his father talked to him, he made him put on
his pajamas and get into bed. And all for that brat of a nurse,
I wonder if she really has orders from the doctors or if she's
that way just to be nasty. But even though I told her, even
though I asked her if she was sure I had to go. You only have

to look at her to realize what she is, with those *femme fatale* airs and that tight apron, a little stinker who thinks she's the directress or something. But no sir, she didn't get off so easy, I gave her a piece of my mind, and on top of that the baby didn't know where to hide he was so ashamed, and his father acted like he didn't understand and must have gotten a good look at her legs while he was at it. The only comforting thing is that the atmosphere is good, you can tell it's a hospital for rich people; the baby has the prettiest night lamp for reading his magazines, and luckily his father remembered to bring his mint candies which are the ones he likes best. But the first thing tomorrow morning I'm going to talk to Doctor de Luisi so he'll put that conceited brat in her place. I wonder if the baby's warm enough with that blanket, just to be sure I'll ask them to leave another one in reach. Of course I'm warm enough, a good thing they finally left, Mama thinks I'm a kid, and she makes me act stupid. A sure thing the nurse is going to think I can't even ask when I need something, the way she looked at me when Mama was arguing with her . . . O.K., they wouldn't let her stay so what are you going to do, I'm big enough now to sleep alone at night, I should think. And anybody should sleep well in this bed, at this hour already you can't hear any noise, sometimes in the distance the hum of the elevator which reminds me of that scary movie that also happened in a hospital, when at midnight the door slowly opened, and the paralytic woman in the bed saw the man in the white mask come in . . .

The nurse is pretty nice, she came back at six-thirty with some papers and began asking me my full name, age, and things like that. I hid the magazine right away because it would have looked better to be reading a real book and not a serial, and I think she realized but didn't say anything, a sure thing she was still angry about what Mama said to her and thinking that I was the same way and that I was going to start giving her orders or something. She asked me if my appendix hurt and I said no, it felt fine that night. "Let's see your pulse," she said, and after taking it she noted something else down on the list and hung it at the foot of the bed. "Are you hungry?" she asked me, and I think I turned red because it took me by surprise that she used the familiar "you," it struck me funny since she's so young and all that. I said I wasn't, although it was a lie because at that hour I'm always hungry. "Tonight you're going to have a very light dinner," she said, and before I could realize she took the package of mint candies away and was gone. I'm not sure if I started to say something, I don't think so. It made me angry that she did that to me as if I were a kid, she could have just as easily told me not to eat candy, but to take them away . . . A sure thing she was furious because of Mama and taking it out on me, out of pure spite; who knows, after she left I got over it right away, I wanted to stay angry with her, but I couldn't. She's so young, I'll bet she's not even nineteen, she must have graduated nursing school just recently. Maybe she's coming to bring me dinner; I'm going to ask her her name, if she's going to be my nurse I have to know her name. But another one came instead, a very friendly lady dressed in blue who brought me broth and biscuits and made me take some green pills. She also asked me my name and how I felt and told me that I would sleep peacefully in this room because it was one of the best in the hospital, and it's true because I slept till almost eight when a little nurse, all wrinkled up like a monkey but very friendly, woke me up, she told me I could get up and wash, but first she gave me a thermometer and told me to put it in like they do in these hospitals, and I didn't understand because at home they put it under your arm, and then she explained and left. Soon Mama came and what a joy to see him looking so well, I was afraid he'd have a sleepless night the poor dear, but kids are like that, so much trouble in the house and then they sleep like a log even though they're far from their Mama who hasn't slept a wink the poor thing. Doctor de Luisi came in to check the baby, and I went outside a moment because he's a big boy now, and I would have enjoyed running into the nurse from yesterday to look her straight in the face and put her in her place just by giving her the once over, but there was nobody in the corridor. Doctor de Luisi came out almost immediately and told me they would operate on the baby the next morning, that he was fine and in the best of conditions for the operation, at his age an appendicitis was nothing. I gratefully thanked him and took the opportunity to tell him that I was very much struck by the afternoon nurse's impertinence, I was telling him this so that my son wouldn't lack the necessary attention. Then I went in to keep the baby company, he was reading his magazines and already knew they were going to operate on him the next day. As if it were the end of the world, the poor thing looks at me so, I'm not going to die, Mama, come on, will you. They took Cacho's appendix out in the hospital and in six days he was ready to play soccer again. Go home and don't worry, I'm fine, I have everything I need. Yes, Mama, yes, ten minutes asking me if it hurts me here or hurts me there, a good thing she has to take care of my sister at home, she finally left and I could finish the serial I'd started last night.

The afternoon nurse's name is Nurse Cora, I asked the little one when she brought me lunch; they gave me very little to eat and green pills again and some mint-flavored drops; it seems those drops make you sleep because the magazines would fall right out of my hands and suddenly I'd be dreaming about school and that we went on a picnic with the girls from teacher's college like last year and we were dancing near the edge of the pool, it was a lot of fun. I woke up around four-thirty and began thinking about the operation, not that I'm afraid, Doctor de Luisi said it's nothing, but the anesthesia must be weird and cutting into you when you're asleep, Cacho said that the worst is waking up, that it hurts a lot, and you might vomit and have fever. The Mama's boy isn't so wise now like he was yesterday, you can see in his face that he's a little afraid, he's such a kid I almost feel sorry for him. He quickly sat up in bed when he saw me come in and hid the magazine under the pillow. The room was a bit cold, and I went to turn up the heat, then I brought the thermometer and gave it to him. "Do you know how to put it in?," I asked him, and his cheeks looked like they were going to burst he got so red. He nodded and stretched out on the bed while I lowered the Venetian blinds and put on the night lamp. When I came over to him so he could give me the thermometer he was still blushing so much that I could hardly keep from laughing, but it's always the same with boys that age, it's hard for them to get used to those things. And to make it worse she looks me in the eyes, why I can't stand that look if after all she's only a woman, I don't know, when I took the thermometer out from under the blankets and handed it to her, she was looking at me and I think she sort of smiled, my getting red must be real noticeable, it's something I can't help, it's stronger than me. Then she noted down my temperature on the sheet at the foot of the bed and left without saying anything. I can hardly remember now what I talked about with Papa and Mama when they came to see me at six. They didn't stay long because Nurse Cora told them I had to be prepared and it was better to keep me calm the night before. I thought Mama was going to let out one of her remarks again but she just looked her up and down, and Papa too but I know the old man's looks, they're something else. Just when she was going I heard Mama say to Miss Cora: "I will thank you to take good care of him, he's a child who's always been very sheltered by his family," or something stupid like that, and I felt like dying I was so angry, I didn't even listen to Nurse Cora's answer, but I'm sure she didn't like it, maybe she thinks I was complaining about her or something.

She came back around six-thirty with one of those little tables on wheels full of bottles and balls of cotton, and I don't know why all of a sudden I felt a little afraid, I really wasn't afraid but I started looking at what was on the little table, all sorts of blue or red bottles, containers of gauze and also forceps and rubber tubes, the poor thing must have started getting scared without his Mama dressed up like a parrot in her Sunday best, I will thank you to take good care of the baby, I've talked to Doctor de Luisi you know, why yes, madam, we're going to treat him like a prince. What a handsome little baby, madam, with that rouge on his cheeks every time he sees me come in. When I pulled back the blankets he made a motion as if to cover himself again, and I think he realized I thought it was funny to see him so prudish. "O.K., lower your pajama pants," I said without looking him in the face. "The pants?", he asked with a voice that cracked like a rooster's. "Yes, of course, the pants," I repeated, and he began to untie the string and unbutton himself with fingers that didn't obey. I had to lower the pants myself to the middle of his thighs, and it was like I had imagined. "You're a pretty big boy already," I said to him, preparing the brush and shaving cream although the truth is he had little to shave. "What do they call you at home?" I asked while I lathered him. "My name's Pablo," he answered with a voice that aroused my pity, he was so ashamed. "But you must have some nickname," I insisted, and it was even worse because it seemed he was going to cry while I shaved off the few little hairs he had there. "So you

don't have any nickname? They just call you the baby,
then." I finished shaving and made a sign for him to cover
himself, but he anticipated it and in a second was covered
to his neck. "Pablo is a nice name," I said to comfort him
a little; I was almost sorry to see him so ashamed, it was the
first time I had to take care of such a shy young boy, but
something in him kept bothering me that perhaps came
from his mother, something stronger than his age that I
didn't like, and even his being so handsome and so well-
developed bothered me, a brat who must already think he's
a man and who would whistle at me the first chance he got.

I closed my eyes, it was the only way to escape a little
from all that, but it did no good because precisely at that
moment she added: "So you don't have any nickname? They
just call you the baby, then" and I could have died, or
grabbed her by the throat and strangled her, and when I
opened my eyes I saw her brown hair almost against my face
because she had bent down to wipe off some leftover shaving
cream, and she smelled of almond shampoo like the one the
drawing teacher uses, or some perfume, and I didn't know
what to say and the only thing that occurred to me was to
ask her: "Your name is Cora, right?" She looked at me
mockingly, with those eyes that already knew me, that had
seen all of me, and said: "Nurse Cora." She said this to
punish me, I know, the same as before when she said:
"You're a pretty big boy already," just to make fun. Although having a red face made me angry, I can never hide
it and it's the worst that can happen to me, so I got up the
courage to say: "You're so young that . . . well, Cora is a very
pretty name." That wasn't what I wanted to say, it was
something else and it seems she realized and it annoyed her,
now I'm sure she's resentful because of Mama. I only
wanted to tell her that she was so young I would have liked
to have been able to call her simply Cora, but how was I
going to say it when at the same moment she got angry and

was already wheeling the table out and I felt like crying, that's another thing I can't prevent, suddenly my voice cracks and everything looks cloudy, just when I have to keep calm to say what I think. She was going out but when she got to the door she stood there a moment as if making sure she hadn't forgotten anything, and I wanted to tell her what I was thinking but I couldn't find the words and the only thing I could think of was to point to the cup of shaving cream, he sat up in bed and after clearing his throat said: "You're forgetting the cup of shaving cream," very seriously and in a grown-up tone. I went back to get the cup, and to calm him a little I ran my hand down his cheek. "Don't worry, Pablito," I said. "It'll all come out fine, the operation is nothing." When I touched him he threw his head back as if offended and then slid down till his mouth was hidden under the edge of the blankets. From there, muffled, he said: "I can call you Cora, right?" I'm too kind, I almost felt sorry for all that shame that was trying to get even somehow, but I knew it wasn't a case for giving in because afterwards it would be difficult to control him, and you've got to control a sick person or it's the same old thing, María Luisa's complications in room fourteen and Doctor de Luisi's scoldings, he has a hound's nose for those things. "Nurse Cora," she said to me taking the cup and leaving. It made me so angry, I felt so much like hitting her, like jumping out of bed and pushing her out, like . . . I don't even understand how I was able to say: "If I were healthy maybe you'd treat me differently." She pretended not to hear, she didn't even turn her head, and I was left alone not feeling like reading or doing anything, deep down I wished she had answered me angrily so I could apologize because that wasn't really what I wanted to say to her, my throat was so choked I don't know how the words got out, I had said it out of pure anger but that wasn't it, or maybe it was but in another way.

The same thing every time, you caress them, say a friendly word, and right then and there the little stud comes out, they don't want to accept that they're still brats. I have to tell Marcial about this, he'll enjoy it and when he sees him on the operating table tomorrow he'll find it even funnier, so delicate the poor thing with that little red face, damn heat that keeps showing through my skin, how can I keep that from happening, maybe breathing deep before speaking, who knows. She must have gone out furious, I'm sure she heard perfectly, I don't know how I said that to her, when I asked her if I could call her Cora she didn't get angry, she said that about Nurse because it's her duty but she wasn't angry, the proof is she came and caressed my face; but no, that was before, first she caressed me and then I said that about Cora and I ruined everything. Now we're worse than before and I won't be able to sleep even if they give me a tube of pills. My belly hurts from time to time, it's strange to run my hand there and feel so smooth, the bad part is that I remember the whole thing again and the almond perfume, Cora's voice, she has such a low voice for such a young and pretty girl, a voice like a bolero singer, something that caresses though she's angry. When I heard footsteps in the corridor I lay down and closed my eyes, I didn't want to see her, I didn't care to see her, I'd rather she leave me in peace, I heard her come in and turn on the overhead light, he pretended to be asleep like a little angel, with a hand covering his face, and he didn't open his eyes until I was beside the bed. When he saw what I brought he turned so red I felt sorry again and a bit like laughing, he was really too idiotic for words. "Come, come, pull your pants down and turn over on the other side," and the poor boy on the verge of kicking and stamping like he'd do with his Mama when he was five years old, I imagine, saying no and crying and getting under the covers and screaming, but the poor thing couldn't do any of that now, he only stared at the enema apparatus and then at me waiting, and suddenly he turned around and began to move his hands under the blankets but couldn't seem to do anything right while I hung the enema bottle on the headboard, I had to pull down the blankets and order him to raise his backside a little so as to slide his pants down more easily and slip a towel under him. "Come on, lift your legs a little, that's right, lie a little more on your face, I said lie more on your face, that's the way." So quiet it was almost as if he were shouting, on the one hand it was funny to be looking at my young admirer's little ass, but again I felt a little sorry for him, it really was as if I were punishing him for what he had said to me. "Tell me if it's too hot," I warned him, but he didn't answer, he must have been biting his fist and I didn't want to see his face, so I sat on the edge of the bed and waited for him to say something, but even though it was a lot of liquid he stood it without a word until the end, and when it was over I said, and this I did say to pay him back for before: "That's what I like, a real little man," and I covered him while I advised him to hold it in as long as possible before going to the bathroom. "Do you want me to put the light out or shall I leave it on till you get up?" she asked me from the door. I don't know how I managed to say it didn't matter, something like that, and I listened to the sound of the door closing and then I covered my head with the blankets and what was I to do, despite the cramps I bit my hands and cried so much that nobody, nobody can imagine how I cried while I cursed her and insulted her and stuck a knife in her chest five, ten, twenty times, cursing her each time and enjoying her suffering and begging me to forgive her for what she had done to me.

It's the same old thing, hey, Suárez, you cut and open, and maybe the big surprise. Of course at his age he has everything in his favor, but just the same I'm going to talk plain to the father, so it won't turn out to be one of those messy affairs. Most probably he'll have a good reaction, but there's something missing there, think of what happened at the beginning of the anesthesia; it's hard to believe it in a kid that age. I went to see him two hours after and found him pretty well considering how long it lasted. When Doctor de Luisi came in I was drying the poor kid's mouth, he wouldn't stop vomiting and he was still under the anesthesia but the doctor examined him with the stethoscope just the same and asked me not to leave his side until he was wide awake. His parents are still in the other room, you can see the good lady isn't used to these things, all of a sudden she stopped showing off, and the old man looks like a regular rag. Go on, Pablito, throw up if you feel like it and moan all you want, I'm here, yes, of course I'm here, the poor thing is still asleep but he grabs my hand as if he were drowning. He must think I'm Mama, they all think that, it's boring. Now Pablo, don't move like that, keep still or it'll hurt more, no, keep your hands down, you can't touch that. The poor thing's having a hard time coming out of the anesthesia, Marcial told me the operation was very long. That's strange, they must have found some complication: sometimes the appendix isn't so visible, I'm going to ask Marcial tonight. Yes, dear, I'm right here, moan all you want but don't move so much, I'm going to wet your lips with this little piece of ice in gauze so you won't be thirsty. Yes, dear, vomit, as much as you want. How strong your hands are, you're going to cover me with bruises, yes, go on, cry if you feel like it, cry, Pablito, that helps, cry and moan, you're so asleep anyway and you think I'm your Mama.

You're real handsome, you know, with that turned up nose and those lashes like curtains, you look older now that you're pale. Now you won't get red for nothing, right, my poor little thing. It hurts, Mama, it hurts, here, let me take off that weight they put on me, I have something on my stomach that weighs so much and hurts, Mama, tell the nurse to take it off. Yes, dear, it'll go away soon, keep still a little, how can you be so strong, I'm going to have to call María Luisa to help me. Come on, Pablo, I'll get angry if you're not still, it's going to hurt much more if you keep moving like that. Ah, it looks like you're starting to get it, it hurts here, Nurse Cora, it hurts so much here, please do something, it hurts so much here, let go of my hands, I can't stand it, Nurse Cora, I can't stand it.

A good thing the poor dear has fallen asleep, the nurse came to get me at two-thirty and told me to stay with him a while, that he was better already, but he looks so pale to me, he must have lost a lot of blood, a good thing Doctor de Luisi said it had turned out well. The nurse was tired from fighting with him, I don't understand why they didn't have me come in before, they're too strict in this hospital. Now it's almost night and the baby has been sleeping all this time, you can see he's exhausted, but he seems to look better, a little more color in his face. He still moans from time to time but he doesn't want to touch the bandage anymore and he's breathing easy, I think he'll have a pretty good night. As if I didn't know my job, but it was inevitable; as soon as the good lady got over her first fright she started coming out with her high and mighty speeches, please be sure all the child's needs are taken care of during the night, Miss. It's a good thing I feel sorry for you, you stupid old bag, if not you'd soon see how I'd treat you. I know this kind, they think that with a good tip the last day they fix everything. And sometimes the tip isn't even that good, but why dwell on it, she's gone and it's all quiet now. Marcial, stay a little, can't you see the boy is sleeping, tell me what happened this morning. O.K., if you're in a hurry we'll leave it for later. No, María Luisa might come in, not here, Marcial. Of course, the boss gets his way, I've already told you I don't want you to kiss me when I'm working, it's not right. As if we didn't have the whole night to kiss, silly. Go. Go on I tell you, or I'll get angry. You big jerk. Yes, dear, see you later. Of course I do. Loads.

It's very dark but just as well, I don't even feel like opening my eyes. It almost doesn't hurt now, how good to breathe slow like this, without that nausea. It's all so quiet, now I remember I saw Mama, she said God knows what, I was feeling so bad. I scarcely looked at the old man, he was at the foot of the bed and winked at me, poor guy, always the same. I feel a bit cold, I'd like another blanket. Nurse Cora, I'd like another blanket. But she was there, as soon as I opened my eyes I saw her sitting by the window reading a magazine. She came over immediately and covered me, I almost didn't have to say anything because she realized right away. I think I mistook her for Mama this afternoon and she was the one who was soothing me, or maybe I was dreaming. Was I dreaming, Nurse Cora? You were holding my hands down, right? I was saying so many silly things, it's just that it hurt a lot, and the nausea . . . I'm sorry, it mustn't be at all nice to be a nurse. Yes, you laugh but I know, maybe I got you dirty and everything. O.K., I won't talk anymore. I'm fine like this, I'm not cold now. No, it doesn't hurt much, only a little. Is it late, Nurse Cora? Sh, you stay nice and quiet now, I've already told you that you can't talk much, be happy it doesn't hurt and stay nice and still. No, it's not late, just seven. Close your eyes and sleep. That's right. Sleep now.

Yes, I would like to but it's not so easy. Every minute

it seems like I'm going to sleep, but suddenly the wound pulls at me or everything goes around in circles in my head, and I have to open my eyes and look at her, she's sitting reading by the window and has put the lamp-shade on so the light won't bother me. Why does she stay here all the time? She has lovely hair, it shines when she moves her head. And she's so young, to think that I mistook her for Mama today, it's crazy. God knows what I said to her, she must have laughed at me again. But she put ice on my mouth, that made me feel so much better, now I remember, she put cologne on my forehead and my hair, and held down my hands so I wouldn't tear the bandage off. She's not angry with me now, maybe Mama apologized or something, she looked at me in another way when she said: "Close your eyes and sleep." I like her to look at me like that, the first day when she took away the candy seems hard to believe. I would like to tell her that she's so pretty, that I don't have anything against her, on the contrary, that I like the fact she's taking care of me at night and not the little nurse. I would like her to put cologne on my hair again. I would like her to apologize to me, to say that I can call her Cora.

He slept for a good while, at eight I figured Doctor de Luisi wouldn't be long so I woke him up to take his temperature. He looked better and it had done him good to sleep. As soon as he saw the thermometer he pulled one hand out of the covers, but I told him to keep still. I didn't want to look him in the eyes so he wouldn't suffer but he got red all the same and began saying he could do it fine on his own. I didn't pay any attention to him, of course, but the poor thing was so tense that I had no choice but to say: "Come, Pablo, you're almost a man now, you're not going to get like that each time, are you?" The same old thing, with his weakness he couldn't hold back the tears; pretending I didn't realize it I noted down the temperature and went to prepare his injection. When she came back I had dried my eyes with the sheet and was so angry with myself that I would have given anything to be able to speak, to tell her it didn't matter, that it really didn't matter but that I couldn't help it. "This doesn't hurt at all," she said to me with the syringe in her hand. "It's just so you'll sleep well the whole night." She uncovered me and again I felt the blood rushing to my face, but she smiled a little and began to rub my thigh with wet cotton. "It doesn't hurt a bit," I said because I had to say something, I couldn't just stay like that while she was looking at me. "You see," she said taking out the needle and rubbing me with the cotton. "You see, it doesn't hurt. Nothing has to hurt you, Pablito." She covered me and ran her hand over my face. I closed my eyes and wanted to be dead, to be dead and for her to run her hand over my face, crying.

I never understood Cora too much but this time she went overboard. I really don't care if I don't understand women, all that matters is that they love you. If they're nervous, if they make a problem out of any silly thing, O.K., baby, it's all right, give me a kiss and that's that. You can see she's still wet behind the ears, it'll be a good while before she learns to live with this damn profession, the poor thing came in tonight with a queer expression on her face and it took me a good half-hour to make her forget that nonsense. She still hasn't found the way to handle some patients, she finally got over the old lady in twenty-two and I thought she would have learned something since then, but now this kid is giving her the headaches again. We were having maté in my room around two in the morning, then she went to give him the injection and when she came back she was in a bad mood, she didn't want to have anything to do with me. She looks good with that angry little sad face, I gradually brought her to, and finally she laughed and told me about it, I like so much to undress her at that hour and feel her tremble a little as if she were cold. It must be late, Marcial. Oh, then I can stay a while longer, he's due for another injection at five-thirty, the little Spanish nurse doesn't come till six. I'm sorry, Marcial, I'm such a fool, worrying about that brat, I know I have him under control but I just feel sorry for him sometimes, they're so silly at that age, so proud, if I could I'd ask Doctor Suárez to switch me, there are two post-operative patients on the second floor, grownups, you can ask them if they've moved their bowels, you hand them the bedpan, you wash them if necessary, and all the while talking about politics or the weather, it's more natural, each one minding his own business, Marcial, not like this, you understand. Yes, of course you've got to adapt to each situation, I'm going to get a lot of boys this age, it's a matter of technique like you say. Yes, dear, of course. But it's just that everything began wrong because of the mother, I haven't forgotten that, you know, from the start there was a kind of misunderstanding, and the boy has his pride and it hurts, especially since he didn't realize what was coming at the beginning and he wanted to play the grownup, to look at me as if he was a man, like you. Now I can't even ask him if he wants to piss, the bad part is he'd be capable of holding it in all night if I stayed in the room. It makes me laugh when I remember, he wanted to say yes but didn't dare, then I got annoyed with all that nonsense and I made him do it so that he'd learn to piss without moving, on his back. He always closes his eyes in those moments but that's almost worse, he's on the verge of crying or of insulting me, one or the other, and he can't, he's so young, Marcial, and that good lady who brought him up like a spoiled brat, the baby this, the baby that, a lot of hats and tailored jackets but deep down the same baby, Mama's precious darling. And then he gets me to top it off, high voltage like you say, when he would have been fine with María Luisa who could be his aunt and who would have washed him every which way without colors rushing to his face. No, frankly, Marcial, I'm just not lucky.

I was dreaming about French class when she turned on the lamp, the first thing I always see is her hair, it must be because she has to bend down for the injections or whatever, her hair near my face, once it tickled me on the mouth and it smells so good and she always smiles a little when she's rubbing me with the cotton, she rubbed a long time before pricking me and I watched that steady hand gradually press the syringe, the yellow liquid that entered slowly, making me ache. "No, it doesn't hurt." I'll never be able to say to her: "It doesn't hurt, Cora." And I'm not going to say Nurse Cora to her, I'm never going to say it, I will speak to her as little as possible and I won't call her Nurse Cora, not even if she gets down on her knees and begs me. No, it doesn't hurt. No, thanks, I feel fine, I'm going back to sleep now. Thanks.

Luckily the color came back to his face but he's still very weak, he could barely give me a kiss, and he almost didn't look at Aunt Esther and she had brought him magazines and a lovely tie for the day we take him home. The morning nurse is a darling, so humble, with her it's a pleasure to talk, she says the baby slept till eight and that he drank a little milk, it seems they're going to start feeding him now, I have to tell Doctor Suárez that cocoa is no good for him, or maybe his father already told him because they were talking for a while. If you could just step out a moment, Madam, we're going to see how this young man is doing.

You stay, Mr. Morán, it's just that all these bandages might upset the mother. Let's see now, my friend. It hurts there? Of course, that's natural. And there, tell me if it hurts there or if it's only sensitive. Good, we're doing fine, pal. And so on for five minutes, if it hurts me here, if I'm sensitive more over there, and the old man looking at my belly as if he was seeing it for the first time. It's strange but I don't feel easy until they go, they're so worried, the poor things, but what can I do, they bother me, they always say what they shouldn't, especially Mama, and a good thing the little nurse makes like she's deaf and puts up with it all with that give-me-a-fat-tip face the poor thing has. Pestering about that cocoa business, as if I was a babe-in-arms. It makes me feel like sleeping five days in a row without seeing anybody, especially Cora, and waking up when it's time to take me home. We might have to wait a few more days, Mr. Morán, you've probably already heard from De Luisi that the operation was more complicated than expected, sometimes there are little surprises. Of course with the constitution your boy has I don't think there'll be any problem, but it would be good to tell the mother that it won't be a matter of a week as we thought at first. Ah, of course, well you'd better speak to the hospital director about that, those are internal problems. Now if it isn't lousy luck, Marcial, I told you so last night, this is going to last longer than we thought. Yes, I know it doesn't matter but you could be a little more understanding, you know very well that tending that boy doesn't make me happy, and him even less, poor kid. Don't give me that look, why shouldn't I feel sorry for him. Don't give me that look.

Nobody forbids me to read but the magazines keep falling out of my hand, and I still have two episodes to go and all that Aunt Esther brought me. My face burns, I must have fever or maybe it's too hot in this room, I'm going to

ask Cora to open the window a little or to take off a blanket.
I would like to sleep, that's what I'd most like, for her to be
sitting there reading a magazine and me sleeping without
seeing her, without knowing she's there, but now she's not
going to stay anymore at night, the worst is over and they'll
leave me by myself. I think I slept a while from three to four,
at five o'clock sharp she came in with a new medicine, some
awful bitter drops. It always seems that she's just bathed and
changed, she's so fresh and she smells of perfumed talcum
powder, of lavender. "This medicine is awful, I know," she
said, and smiled to pick up my spirits. "No, it's a little bitter,
that's all," I said to her. "How did you do today?," she asked,
shaking the thermometer. I said fine, I slept, Doctor Suárez
found me better, it didn't hurt as much. "Well, then here's
a little work," she said, giving me the thermometer. I didn't
know what to answer and she went to close the blinds and
tidied up the bottles on the little table while I took my
temperature. I even had time to look at the thermometer
before she came for it. "Why, I've got quite a fever," he said
looking scared. It was inevitable, I'll never learn, to get him
out of a tight spot I give him the thermometer and naturally
the baby doesn't lose a minute in finding out that he's flying
with fever. "It's always the same the first four days, and
besides nobody asked you to look," I said to him, more
furious with myself than him. I asked him if he'd moved his
bowels and he said no. His face was sweating, I dried it and
put on a little cologne; he had closed his eyes before answering me and he didn't open them while I combed him a little
so that the hair on his forehead wouldn't bother him. One
hundred and three point eight really was a lot of fever. "Try
to sleep a while," I said, figuring out at what time I could
call Doctor Suárez. Without opening his eyes he made a
gesture as if annoyed, and enunciating each word he said:
"You're not nice to me, Cora." I couldn't find an answer,

I stayed beside him until he opened his eyes and looked at me with all his fever and all his sadness. Almost without realizing I put out my hand and tried to caress his forehead, but he slapped it away and something in the wound must have pulled at him because he twitched with pain. Before I could react he said very quietly, "You wouldn't be this way with me if you had met me elsewhere." I almost laughed, but it was so ridiculous when he said that while his eyes filled with tears that the same old thing happened to me, he made me angry and almost afraid, I suddenly felt unprotected before that pretentious little boy. I managed to control myself (I owe that to Marcial, he taught me self-control and I'm better at it each time) and I straightened up as if nothing had happened, put the towel on the hook, and closed the bottle of cologne. Well, now we knew where we stood, in the end it was much better like this. Nurse, patient, and that's all there is to it. Let his mother put on the cologne, I had other things to do to him and I'd do them without further thought. I don't know why I stayed more than was necessary. Marcial said when I told him about it that I had wanted to give him the chance to apologize, to beg my pardon, I don't know, maybe it was that or something different, maybe I stayed so he would keep insulting me, to see how far he'd go. But he kept his eyes shut and the sweat soaked his forehead and cheeks, it was as if they'd put me in boiling water, I saw red and purple spots when I squeezed my eyes shut to not look at her, knowing she was still there, and I would have given anything for her to bend down and dry my forehead again as if I hadn't said that to her, but now it was impossible, she would go and not do anything, not say anything to me, and I would open my eyes and find the night, the lamp, the empty room, a little perfume still, and I would repeat to myself ten times, one hundred times, that I had done well to say what I had said to her, so that she'd learn, so that she wouldn't treat me like a boy, so that she would leave me in peace, so that she wouldn't go.

They always start at the same hour, between six and seven in the morning, it must be a couple nesting on the ledges around the patio, a pigeon chirping and the female pigeon answering him, I said to the little nurse who comes to wash me and give me breakfast, she shrugged her shoulders and said that other patients had complained about the pigeons before but the director didn't want to get rid of them. I don't even know how long I've been hearing them anymore, the first mornings I was too sleepy or in too much pain to notice, but for three days now I've been listening to the pigeons and they make me sad, I would like to be home hearing Milord bark, hearing Aunt Esther get up at that hour to go to Mass. Damn fever that never goes down, they'll keep me here until God knows when, I'm going to ask Doctor Suárez this morning, after all I'd be perfectly fine at home. Look, Mr. Morán, I want to be frank with you, the picture isn't at all simple. No, Nurse Cora, I prefer you to stay with that patient and I'll tell you why. But, Marcial, tell me . . . Come, I'll make you a nice strong cup of coffee, how green you still are, you should be ashamed of yourself. Now listen, honey, I've been talking to Doctor Suárez, and it seems that the kid . . .

Luckily they quiet down afterward, maybe they go flying, all over the city, pigeons are lucky. What an endless morning, I was happy when the old folks left, now since I have so much fever it's gotten into them to come more often. Well, if I have to stay here four or five days more, what does it matter. It would be better at home, of course, but I'd still have fever and I'd feel just as bad. To think that

I can't even look at a magazine, it's a weakness as if I had
no blood left. But it's all because of the fever, Doctor de
Luisi told me last night and Doctor Suárez repeated it this
morning, they know. I sleep a lot but it's as if time didn't
pass, it's always before three as if I cared if it was three or
five o'clock. On the contrary, at three the little nurse goes
and it's a pity because with her I'm fine. If I could sleep in
one long stretch till midnight it would be much better.
Pablo, it's me, Nurse Cora. Your night nurse who hurts you
with injections. I know, I know it doesn't hurt, silly, I'm only
joking. Sleep some more if you want, that's fine. He said
"Thanks" without opening his eyes, but he could have
opened them, I know he was chatting with the little Spanish
nurse at noon although they've forbidden him to talk a lot.
Before going I turned suddenly and he was looking at me,
I felt all the time he had been looking at me from behind.
I came back and sat on the edge of the bed, I took his pulse,
I arranged his sheets that he had creased with his feverish
hands. He looked at my hair, then lowered his eyes and
avoided mine. I went to get what I needed to prepare him
and he let me without a word, his eyes fixed on the window,
ignoring me. They'd come for him at exactly five-thirty, he
still had a while left to sleep, his parents were waiting on the
ground floor because it would have upset him to see them
at that hour. Doctor Suárez was going to come a bit before
to explain to him that they had to complete the operation,
anything that wouldn't upset him too much. But instead
they sent Marcial, it took me by surprise to see him come
in like that but he made a sign to me not to move and
remained at the foot of the bed reading the temperature
sheet until Pablo got used to his presence. He began talking
to him a little jokingly, he led the conversation as only he
knows how, the cold outside, how cozy it was in that room,
and he was looking at him not saying anything, as if waiting,

while I felt so strange, I kept wishing Marcial would go and leave me alone with him, I could have told him better than anybody, although perhaps not, probably not. I know, Doctor, they're going to operate on me again, you're the one who gave me the anesthesia last time, oh well, better that than staying in this bed with this fever. I knew they'd finally have to do something, why does it hurt so much since yesterday, a different pain, from further in. And you, sitting there, don't make that face, don't smile as if you were coming to invite me out to the movies. Go with him and kiss him in the corridor, I wasn't so asleep the other evening when you got angry with him because he had kissed you here. Go, the two of you, let me sleep, sleeping it doesn't hurt so much.

O.K. now, kid, we're going to get this matter over with once and for all, how long do you think you can occupy our bed here, huh? Count nice and slow, one, two, three. That's fine, you keep counting and in a week you'll be home eating a juicy steak. Barely a quarter of an hour, baby, and he was sewed up again. You should have seen De Luisi's face, one never gets completely used to these things. Hey listen, I took the opportunity to ask Suárez to relieve you like you wanted, I told him you were worn out from such a serious case; maybe they'll send you to the second floor if you talk to him, too. O.K., do what you like, all that complaining the other night and now you're the Good Samaritan. Don't get angry at me, I did it for you. Yes, of course he did it for me but it was a waste of time, I'm staying with him tonight and every night. He started waking up at eight-thirty, his parents left immediately because it was better not to see the way they looked, poor things, and when Doctor Suárez arrived he asked me in a whisper if I wanted María Luisa to relieve me, but I made a sign that I was staying and he left. María Luisa stayed with me for a while because we had to hold him down and soothe him, then he relaxed suddenly and hardly vomited, he's so weak he went back to sleep moaning very little until ten. It's the pigeons, you'll see, Mama, they're already billing and cooing like every morning, I don't know why they don't shoo them away, let them fly to another tree. Let me hold your hand, Mama, I feel so cold. Oh, then I was dreaming, it seemed it was already morning and that the pigeons were there. I'm sorry, I thought you were Mama. Again he avoided my eyes and got mad, again he put all the blame on me. I tended him as if I didn't realize he was still angry, I sat beside him and wet his lips with ice. When he looked at me, after I put cologne on his hands and forehead, I came closer and smiled. "Call me Cora," I said. "I know we didn't get along at first, but we're going to be such good friends, Pablo." He looked at me, silent. "Say to me: 'Yes, Cora.'" He kept looking at me. "Nurse Cora," he said finally, and closed his eyes. "No, Pablo, no," I begged him, kissing his cheek, close to his mouth. "I'm going to be Cora for you, and for you only." I had to sit back, but he spattered my face just the same. I dried him, held up his head so that he could rinse his mouth, I kissed him again, talking into his ear. "I'm sorry," he said faintly, "I couldn't hold it back." I told him don't be silly, that's what I was there for, to take care of him, he should vomit all he wanted to relieve himself. "I would like Mama to come," he said to me, looking away with empty eyes. I still caressed his hair a little, I tidied his blankets, waiting for him to say something, but he was very distant, and I felt I would make him suffer still more if I stayed. At the door I turned and waited, his eyes were wide open, fixed on the ceiling. "Pablito," I said. "Please, Pablito. Please, dear." I returned to the bed, bent down to kiss him, he smelled cold, behind the cologne was vomit, anesthesia. If I stayed a second more I would have cried in front of him, for him. I kissed him again and ran out, I went down to get his mother and María Luisa; I didn't want to return while his mother was there, at least that night I didn't want to return and afterwards I knew too well that there was no need to return to that room, that Marcial and María Luisa would take care of everything until the room was free again.

THE ISLAND AT NOON

THE FIRST TIME he saw the island, Marini was politely leaning over the seats on the left, adjusting a plastic table before setting a lunch tray down. The passenger had looked at him several times as he came and went with magazines or glasses of whisky; Marini lingered while he adjusted the table, wondering, bored, if it was worth responding to the passenger's insistent look, one American woman out of many, when in the blue oval of the window appeared the coast of the island, the golden strip of the beach, the hills that rose toward the desolate plateau. Correcting the faulty position of the glass of beer, Marini smiled to the passenger. "The Greek islands," he said. "Oh, yes, Greece," the American woman answered with false interest. A bell rang briefly, and the steward straightened up, without removing the professional smile from his thin lips. He began attending to a Syrian couple, who ordered tomato juice, but in the tail of the plane he gave himself a few seconds to look down again; the island was small and solitary, and the Aegean Sea surrounded it with an intense blue that exalted the curl of a dazzling and kind of petrified white, which down below would be foam breaking against reefs and coves. Marini saw that the deserted beaches ran north and west; the rest was the mountain which fell straight into the sea. A rocky and deserted island, although the lead-gray spot near the northern beach could be a house, perhaps a group of primitive houses. He started opening the can of juice, and when he had straightened up the island had vanished from the window; only the sea was left, an endless green horizon. He looked at his wrist-watch without knowing why; it was exactly noon.

Marini liked being assigned to the Rome-Teheran line. The flight was less gloomy than on the northern lines, and the girls seemed happy to go to the Orient or to get to know Italy. Four days later, while he was helping a little boy who had lost his spoon and was pointing downheartedly at his dessert plate, he again discovered the edge of the island. There was a difference of eight minutes, but when he leaned over to a window in the tail he had no doubts; the island had an unmistakable shape, like a turtle whose paws were barely out of the water. He looked at it until they called for him, this time sure that the lead-gray spot was a group of houses; he managed to make out the lines of some cultivated fields that extended to the beach. During the stop at Beirut he looked at the stewardess's atlas and wondered if the island wasn't Horos. The radio operator, an indifferent Frenchman, was surprised at his interest. "All those islands look alike. I've been doing this route for two years, and I don't care a fig about them. Yes, show it to me next time." It wasn't Horos but Xiros, one of the many islands on the fringe of the tourist circuits. "It won't last five years," the stewardess said to him while they had a drink in Rome. "Hurry up if you're thinking of going, the hordes will be there any moment now. Genghis Cook is watching." But Marini kept thinking about the island, looking at it when he remembered or if there was a window near, almost always shrugging his shoulders in the end. None of it made any sense—flying three times a week at noon over Xiros was as unreal as dreaming three times a week that he was flying over Xiros. Everything was falsified in the futile and recurrent vision; except, perhaps, the desire to repeat it, the consulting of the wristwatch before noon, the brief, pricking contact with the dazzling white band at the edge of an almost black blue, and the houses where the fishermen would barely lift their eyes to follow the passage of that other unreality.

Eight or nine weeks later, when they offered him the New York run, with all its advantages, Marini thought it was the chance to end that innocent and annoying obsession. In his pocket he had a guide book in which an imprecise geographer with a Levantine name gave more details about Xiros than was usual. He answered no, hearing himself as from a distance, and, avoiding the shocked surprise of a boss and two secretaries, he went to have a bite in the company's canteen, where Carla was waiting for him. Carla's bewildered disappointment did not disturb him; the southern coast of Xiros was uninhabitable, but toward the west remained traces of a Lydian or perhaps Creto-Mycenaean colony, and Professor Goldmann had found two stones carved with hieroglyphics that the fishermen used as piles for the small dock. Carla's head ached, and she left almost immediately; octopus was the principal resource for the handful of inhabitants, every five days a boat arrived to load the fish and leave some provisions and materials. In the travel agency they told him he would have to charter a special boat from Rynos, or perhaps it would be possible to go in the small boat that picked up the octupuses, but

Marini could find out about this only in Rynos, where the agency didn't have an agent. At any rate, the idea of spending a few days on the island was just a plan for his June vacation; in the weeks that followed he had to replace White on the Tunis run, and then there was a strike, and Carla went back to her sisters' house in Palermo. Marini went to live in a hotel near the Piazza Navona, where there were secondhand bookstores; he amused himself not very enthusiastically by looking for books on Greece, and from time to time he leafed through a conversation manual. The word *kalimera* pleased him, and he tried it out on a redhead in a cabaret; he went to bed with her, learned about her grandfather in Odos and about certain unaccountable sore throats. In Rome it rained, in Beirut Tania was always waiting for him; there were other stories, always relatives or sore throats; one day it was again the Teheran run, the island at noon. Marini stayed glued to the window so long that the new stewardess considered him a poor partner and let him know how many trays she had served. That night Marini invited the stewardess for dinner at the Firouz, and it wasn't difficult to make her forgive him for the morning's distraction. Lucía advised him to have his hair cut American-style; he talked to her about Xiros for a while, but later he realized she preferred the vodka-lime of the Hilton. Time passed in things like that, in infinite trays of food, each one with the smile to which the passenger had the right. On the return trips the plane flew over Xiros at eight in the morning; the sun glared against the larboard windows, and you could scarcely see the golden turtle; Marini preferred to wait for the noons of the trip going, knowing that then he could stay a long minute against the window, while Lucía (and then Felisa) somewhat ironically took care of things. Once he took a picture of Xiros, but it came out blurred; he already knew some things about the island, he had underlined the rare mentions in a couple of books. Felisa told him that the pilots called him the madman of the island, but that didn't bother him. Carla had just written that she had decided not to have the baby, and Marini sent her two weeks' wages and thought that the rest would not be enough for his vacation. Carla accepted the money and let him know through a friend that she'd probably marry the dentist from Treviso. Everything had such little importance at noon, on Mondays and Thursdays and Saturdays (twice a month on Sundays).

As time went on, he began to realize that Felisa was the only one who understood him a little; there was a tacit agreement that she would take care of the flight at noon, as soon as he stationed himself by the tail window. The island was visible for a few minutes, but the air was always so clean, and it was outlined by the sea with such a minute cruelty that the smallest details were implacably adjusted to the memory of the preceding flight: the green spot of the head-land to the north, the lead-gray houses, the nets drying on the sand. When the nets weren't there, Marini felt as if he had been robbed, insulted. He thought of filming the passage over the island, to repeat the image in the hotel, but he preferred to save the money on the camera since there was less than a month left for vacation. He didn't keep a very strict account of the days; sometimes it was Tania in Beirut, sometimes Felisa in Teheran, almost always his younger brother in Rome, all a bit blurred, amiably easy and cordial and as if replacing something else, filling the hours before or after the flight, and during the flight, everything, too, was blurred and easy and stupid until it was time to lean toward the tail window, to feel the cold crystal like the boundary of an aquarium, where the golden turtle slowly moved in the thick blue.

That day, the nets were clearly sketched on the sand, and Marini could have sworn that the black dot on the left, at the edge of the sea, was a fisherman who must have been looking at the plane. *"Kalimera,"* he absurdly thought. It no longer made any sense to wait. Mario Merolis would lend him the money he needed for the trip, and in less than three days he would be in Xiros. With his lips against the window, he smiled, thinking that he would climb to the green spot, that he would enter the sea of the northern coves naked, that he would fish octopuses with the men, communicating through signs and laughter. Nothing was difficult once decided—a night train, the first boat, another old and dirty boat, the night on the bridge, close to the stars, the taste of *anis* and mutton, daybreak among the islands. He landed with the first lights, and the captain introduced him to an old man, probably the elder. Klaios took his left hand and spoke slowly, looking him in the eyes. Two boys came, and Marini found out that they were Klaios' sons. The captain of the small boat exhausted his English: Twenty inhabitants, octopus, fish, five houses, Italian visitor would pay lodging Klaios. The boys laughed when Klaios discussed drachmas; Marini, too, already friends with the younger boys, watching the sun come up over a sea not as dark as from the air, a poor, clean room, a pitcher of water, smell of sage and tanned hides.

They left him alone to go load the small boat, and after tearing off his traveling clothes and putting on bathing trunks and sandals, he set out for a walk on the island. You still couldn't see anybody; the sun slowly but surely rose, and from the thickets grew a subtle smell, slightly acidic, mixing with the iodine of the wind. It must have been ten when he reached the northern headland and recognized the largest of the coves. He preferred being alone, although he would have liked to bathe at the sand beach even better; the island impregnated him, and he enjoyed it with such intimacy that he was incapable of thinking or choosing. His skin burned from sun and wind when he undressed to thrust himself into the sea from a rock; the water was cold and did him good. He let a sly current carry him to the entrance of a grotto, he returned to the open sea, rolled over on his back, accepted it all in a single act of conciliation that was also a name for the future. He knew without the slightest doubt that he would not leave the island, that somehow he would stay forever on the island. He managed to imagine his brother, Felisa, their faces when they found out he had stayed to live off fishing on a large solitary rock. He had already forgotten them when he turned over to swim toward the shore.

The sun dried him immediately, and he went down toward the houses, where two astonished women looked at him before running inside and closing their doors. He waved a greeting in the void and walked down toward the nets. One of Klaios' sons was waiting for him on the beach, and Marini pointed to the sea, inviting him. The boy hesitated, pointing to his cloth pants and red shirt. Then he ran toward one of the houses and came back almost naked; they dived together into an already lukewarm sea, dazzling under the eleven o'clock sun.

Drying himself in the sand, Ionas began to name things. *"Kalimera,"* Marini said, and the boy doubled over with laughter. Then Marini repeated the new sentences, teaching Ionas Italian words. Almost on the horizon the small boat grew smaller and smaller; Marini felt that now he was really alone on the island with Klaios and his people. He would let some days pass, he would pay for his room and learn to fish; some afternoon, when they were well acquainted, he would talk to them about staying and working with them. Getting up, he held out his hand to Ionas and started walking slowly toward the hill. The slope was steep, and he savored each pause, turning around time and again to look at the nets on the beach, the figures of the women speaking gaily to Ionas and Klaios and looking at him askance, laughing. When he reached the green spot he entered a world where the smell of thyme and sage were one with the fire of the sun and the sea breeze. Marini looked at his wrist watch and then, with an impatient gesture, put it in the pocket of his bathing trunks. It wouldn't be easy to kill the former man, but there up high, tense with sun and space, he felt the enterprise was possible. He was in Xiros, he was there where he had so often doubted he could reach. He let himself fall back among the hot stones, he endured their edges and inflamed ridges and looked vertically at the sky; far away he could hear the hum of an engine.

Closing his eyes, he told himself he wouldn't look at the plane; he wouldn't let himself be contaminated by the worst of him that once more was going to pass over the island. But in the shadows of his eyelids he imagined Felisa with the trays, in that very moment distributing the trays, and his replacement, perhaps Giorgio or someone new from another line, someone who would also be smiling as he served the wine or the coffee. Unable to fight against all that past he opened his eyes and sat up, and in the same moment saw the right wing of the plane, almost over his head, tilt unaccountably, the changed sound of the jet engines, the almost vertical drop into the sea. He rushed down the hill, knocking against rocks and lacerating his arm among thorns. The island hid the place of the fall from him, but he turned before reaching the beach and through a predictable short-cut he passed the first ridge of the hill and came out onto the smaller beach. The plane's tail was sinking some 100 yards away, in total silence. Marini ran and dived into the water, still waiting for the plane to come up to float; but all you could see was the soft line of the waves, a cardboard box bobbing absurdly near the place of the fall, and almost at the end, when it no longer made sense to keep swimming, a hand out of the water, just for a second, enough time for Marini to change direction and dive under to catch by his hair the man who struggled to hold onto him and hoarsely swallowed air that Marini let him breathe without getting too close. Towing him little by little he got him to the shore, took the body dressed in white in his arms, and laying him on the sand he looked at the face full of foam where death had already settled, bleeding through an enormous gash in his throat. What good was artificial respiration if, with each convulsion, the gash seemed to open a little more and was like a repugnant mouth that called to Marini, tore him from his little happiness of such few hours on the island, shouted to him between torrents something he was no longer able to hear? Klaios' sons came running and behind them the women. When Klaios arrived, the boys gathered around the body lying on the sand, unable to understand how he had had the strength to swim to shore and drag himself there bleeding. "Close his eyes," one of the women begged crying. Klaios looked toward the sea, searching for other survivors. But, as always, they were alone on the island, and the open-eyed corpse was all that was new between them and the sea.

Instructions For John Howell

For Peter Brook.

Thinking about it afterwards—on the street, in a train, crossing fields—all that would have seemed absurd, but what is theater but a compromise with the absurd and its most efficient, lavish practice? Rice, who was bored on an autumnal London weekend and had entered the Aldwych without taking too close a look at the program, found the first act of the play, above all, mediocre; the absurd began at intermission, when the man in grey came over to his seat and politely invited him, with an almost inaudible voice, to accompany him backstage. Not too surprised, he thought the management of the theater must be doing a questionnaire, some vague investigation for publicity purposes. "If it's about an opinion," Rice said, "the first act seemed wishy-washy to me, and the lighting for example . . ." The man in grey agreed amiably, but his hand kept pointing to a side exit, and Rice realized that he should get up and accompany him without having to be begged. "I would have preferred

[99]

a cup of tea," he thought while he walked down some steps to a side aisle and let himself be led, half-absently, half-annoyed. Almost abruptly, he found himself before a wing with scenery representing the library of a middle-class house; two bored-looking men greeted him as if his visit had been expected or even taken for granted. "You'll do marvelously," said the taller of the two. The other man bowed his head, looking like a mute. "We don't have much time," the tall man said, "but I'll try to explain your role in two words." He talked mechanically, almost as if he ignored Rice's real presence and limited himself to carrying out a monotonous assignment. "I don't understand," Rice said, taking a step back. "It's almost better," the tall man said. "In these cases, analyzing puts you rather at a disadvantage; you'll see, as soon as you get used to the lights, you'll start enjoying it. You already know the first act; I know, you didn't like it. Nobody likes it. It's from now on that the play can get better. It depends, of course." "Let's hope it gets better," said Rice, who thought he had misunderstood, "but in any case it's time for me to get back to my seat." As he had taken another step back, the mild resistance of the man in grey, who murmured an "Excuse me" without moving aside, didn't surprise him too much. "It seems we don't understand each other," the tall man said, "which is a pity, because there are only four minutes to go before the second act. Please listen carefully. You are Howell, Eva's husband. You've already seen that Eva is unfaithful to Howell with Michael, and that Howell has probably realized, although he prefers to keep quiet for reasons that are still not clear. Don't move, please, it's simply a wig." But the warning seemed almost useless, since the man in grey and the mute man had taken him by the arms, and a tall, thin girl, who had suddenly appeared, was fitting something warm on his head. "You won't want me to start shouting and causing an uproar in the theater," said Rice, trying to control the tremor in his voice. The tall man shrugged his shoulders. "You wouldn't do that," he said wearily. "It would be so gauche . . . No, I'm sure you wouldn't do that. Besides, the wig looks good on you, you look like a redhead." Knowing he shouldn't say this, Rice said: "But I'm not an actor." All of them, even the girl, smiled encouragement. "Precisely," said the tall man. "You are well aware of the difference. You are not an actor; you are Howell. When you go out onto the stage, Eva will be in the drawing room writing a letter to Michael. You will pretend not to realize that she hides the paper and conceals her uneasiness. From that moment on, do what you like. The glasses, Ruth." "What I like?" said Rice, trying soundlessly to free his arms, while Ruth adjusted a pair of horn-rimmed glasses on him. "Yes, that's what it's about," the tall man said listlessly, and Rice vaguely suspected that he was fed up with repeating the same things every night. The bell started ringing for the audience, and Rice managed to make out the movements of the stagehands on the stage, some changing of lights; Ruth had suddenly disappeared. An indignation, more bitter than violent, that somehow seemed out of place, came over him. "This is a stupid farce," he said trying to break loose, "and I'm warning you . . ." "I'm sorry," the tall man murmured. "Frankly I would have thought differently of you. But since you're taking it like this . . ." It wasn't exactly a threat, although the three men surrounded him in a way that demanded obedience or an out-and-out struggle; it seemed to Rice that one thing would have been as absurd or as false as the other. "Howell enters now," said the tall man, showing him the narrow passage between the wings. "Once you're there, do what you like, but we would be sorry if . . ." He said it amiably, without disturbing the sudden silence of the hall; the curtain rose with a stroking of velvet, and they received a whiff of warm air. "If I were you, I'd think it over, however," the tall man added wearily. "Go, now." Pushing him without pushing him, the three accompanied him to the middle of the wings. A violet light blinded Rice; in front was a space that seemed infinite, and to the left he guessed the great cavern, something like a gigantic contained breath, which, after all, was the real world, where white shirt fronts and perhaps hats or upsweeps were gradually taking shape. He took a step or two, feeling that his legs weren't responding, and was about to turn around and rush back when Eva, hurriedly rising, came forward and offered him her hand, which seemed to float in the violet light at the end of a very white and long arm. The hand was icy, and Rice had the impression that it twitched a little in his. Letting her lead him to the center of the set, he confusedly listened to Eva's explanations about her headache, her preference for the soft light and peacefulness of the library, waiting for her silence to then step to the forestage and announce, in two words, that they were being swindled. But Eva seemed to be waiting for him to sit on a sofa of as dubious taste as the plot and the set, and Rice realized that it was impossible, almost grotesque, to keep standing while she, holding out her hand again, repeated the invitation with a weary smile. From the sofa, he could see the first rows of the stalls better, scarcely separated from the stage by the light, which had been turning from violet to a yellowish orange, but curiously it was easier for Rice to turn toward Eva and withstand her gaze which in some way still bound him to that foolishness, putting off for another second the only decision possible without accepting madness and yielding to sham. "These autumn afternoons are endless," Eva had said, looking for a white metal box among the books and papers on the low table and offering him a cigarette. Mechanically, Rice took out his lighter, feeling more and more ridiculous with the wig and glasses; but the minor ritual of lighting the cigarettes and inhaling the first whiffs was like a truce. It permitted him to sit more comfortably, relaxing the unbearable tension of his body that knew it was being looked at by cold and invisible constellations. He heard his answers to Eva's sentences; the words seemed to bring each other to life with little effort, without their having to talk about anything concrete—a house of cards dialogue, in which Eva was putting up the walls of the fragile building, and Rice effortlessly intercalated his own cards until, when finishing a long-winded explanation which included Michael's name ("You've already seen that Eva is unfaithful to Howell with Michael") and other names and places, a tea party which Michael's mother had attended (or was it Eva's mother?) and an anxious justification and almost on the verge of tears, with a gesture of anxious hope, Eva leaned toward Rice as if she wished to embrace him or wait for him to take her in his arms, and, exactly after the last word said in a very clear voice, she murmured near Rice's ear: "Don't let them kill me," and without transition returned to her professional voice to complain about being lonely and abandoned. There was a knock on the door in the background, and Eva bit her lip as if she had wanted to add something more (but Rice thought of that, too confused to react in time), and stood up to welcome Michael, who came in with the false smile he had worn so unbearably during the first act. A lady dressed in red, an old man—suddenly the stage was populated with people exchanging greetings, flowers, and news. Rice shook the hands held out to him and sat down on the sofa again as soon as possible, shielding himself behind another cigarette; now the action seemed to go on without him, and the audience received with satisfied murmurs a series of brilliant word plays from Michael and the other character actors, while Eva attended to the tea and gave the servant instructions. Perhaps it was the moment to approach the front of the stage, drop the cigarette, and crush it with his foot, in time to announce: "Dear audience . . ." But maybe it would be more elegant *(Don't let them kill me)* to wait for the curtain's fall and then, quickly stepping forward, reveal the fraud. In all of this, there was a kind of ceremonial which wasn't difficult to heed; awaiting his hour, Rice entered into the dialogue proposed by the old gentleman, accepted the cup of tea Eva offered him without looking her in the face, as if she knew Michael and the lady in red were watching her. The thing was to resist, to face up to a time endlessly tense, to be stronger than the awkward coalition that aspired to turn him into a puppet. Already he could tell how the words directed to him (sometimes by Michael, sometimes the lady in red, almost never Eva, now) implicitly carried the reply; if the puppet answered what was expected, the play could continue. Rice thought that if he had only had a little more time to master the situation, it would have been fun to answer against the grain and put the actors in tight spots, but they would not tolerate it; his false freedom of action would permit only wild rebellion, riot. *Don't let them kill me,* Eva had said; somehow, as absurd as all the rest, Rice kept feeling that it was better to wait. The curtain fell upon a sententious and bitter repartee by the lady in red, and to Rice, the actors seemed like figures who suddenly stepped down an invisible step: Diminished, indifferent (Michael shrugged his shoulders, turning around and heading backstage), they all left the stage without looking at each other, but Rice noticed that Eva turned her head toward him while the lady in red and the old man lead her amiably by the arm toward the right wings. He thought of following her, had the vague hope of a dressing room and private conversation. "Magnificent," said the tall man, patting him on the shoulder. "Very good, a very good job indeed." He pointed toward the curtain letting the last applause pass through. "They really liked it. Let's have a drink." The other two men were somewhat further away, smiling amiably, and Rice gave up the idea of following Eva. The tall man opened a door at the end of the first corridor, and they entered a small parlor where there were ramshackle chairs, a wardrobe, an already opened bottle of whisky, and beautiful crystal glasses. "You've done a good job," the tall man insisted, while they sat around Rice. "A little ice, right? Of course, anybody's throat would be dry." Before he could say no, the man in grey handed Rice an almost full glass. "The third act is more difficult, but also more fun for Howell," the tall man said. "You've already seen how they gradually reveal the games." He began to explain the plot, nimbly, without hesitation. "You've complicated matters in a way," he said, "I never imagined you would act so passively with your wife; I would have reacted otherwise." "How?" Rice asked dryly. "Ah, dear friend, it's not right to ask that. My opinion could alter your own decisions, since you must have a preconceived plan by now. Or don't you?" As Rice was silent, he added: "I say this precisely because it's not a matter of having preconceived plans. We are all too satisfied to risk failing with the rest." Rice drank down a long gulp of whisky. "But you told me I could do what I wanted in the second act," he remarked. The man in grey started to laugh, but the tall man gave him a look, and the other made a quick gesture of apology. "There's a margin for adventure or chance—whichever you prefer," said the tall man. "But from now on please pay attention to what I indicate, always given, of course, that you have absolute freedom as to detail." His right hand opened with the palm upward; he looked steadily at it while the index finger of the other hand rested upon it again and again. Between two gulps (they had filled his glass again), Rice listened to the instructions for John Howell. Sustained by alcohol and by something that was like a slow turning inward which filled him with cold anger, he effortlessly discovered the meaning of the instructions, the preparation of the plot which would come to a crisis in the last act. "I hope it is clear," the tall man said, making a circular movement with his finger in the palm of his hand. "It is very clear," said Rice getting up, "but I'd also like to know if in the fourth act . . ." "Let us not confuse the issue, dear friend," the tall man said. "In the next intermission, we'll come back to this, but now I suggest that you concentrate exclusively on the third act. Ah, the street clothes, please." Rice felt the mute man unbuttoning his jacket; the man in grey had taken a tweed suit and gloves out of the wardrobe; mechanically, Rice changed outfits under the approving eyes of the three. The tall man had opened the door and was waiting; far away you could hear the bell. "This damn wig makes me hot," thought Rice, finishing the whisky in one gulp. Almost immediately, he found himself between new wings, without resisting the friendly pressure of a hand on his elbow. "Not yet," said the tall man, behind him. "Remember that it's cool in the park. Perhaps if you raised the collar of your jacket . . . Let's go, it's your cue." From a bench on the edge of the path Michael came toward him, greeting him with a joke. He was supposed to respond passively and discuss the merits of autumn in Regent's Park, until Eva and the lady in red, who must be feeding the swans, arrived. For the first time—it surprised him as much as the others—Rice accentuated his words in an allusion that the audience seemed to appreciate and which obliged Michael to put himself on the defensive, forcing him to use the most visible recourses of the profession to find a way out. Turning his back on him while he lit a cigarette, as if he wanted to protect himself from the wind, Rice looked over the top of his glasses and saw the three men backstage, the tall man's arm making a threatening gesture. He laughed between his teeth (he must have been a little drunk, and besides he was having a good time, and the waving arm was extremely funny to him) before turning around and resting a hand on Michael's shoulder. "You see funny things in parks," said Rice. "Really I don't understand how you can waste time with swans and lovers when you're in a London park." The audience laughed more than Michael, excessively concerned with the arrival of Eva and the lady in red. Unswervingly, Rice continued against the tide, little by little violating the instructions in a ferocious and absurd fencing match against very capable actors who were trying really hard to make him return to his role, and at times they succeeded, but he'd escape them again to somehow help Eva, not really knowing why but thinking (and this made him laugh, and it must have been the whisky) that all he had changed in that moment would inevitably alter the last act *(Don't let them kill me).* And the others had realized his purpose, because it was enough to look over his glasses toward the wings on the left to see the tall man's angry gestures. On stage and off, they were fighting against him and Eva; they'd get between them so that they couldn't communicate, so that she couldn't talk to him. And now the old gentleman arrived, followed by a gloomy chauffeur. There was a brief moment of calm (Rice remembered the instructions: a pause, then the conversation on buying shares, then the lady in red's revealing words, and curtain), and in that interval, in which Michael and the lady in red had to move aside so that the gentleman could talk to Eva and Howell about stock market strategy (really, they didn't leave anything out of this play), the pleasure of spoiling the action a little more filled Rice with something that seemed like happiness. With a gesture that made the profound scorn he felt for these risky speculations very clear, he took Eva

by the arm, cleverly eluded the furious and smiling gentleman's engaging maneuver, and walked with her, hearing
behind him a wall of ingenious words which didn't concern
him, exclusively invented for the audience, and meanwhile
Eva, meanwhile a warm breath hardly a second against his
cheek, the light murmur of her real voice saying: "Stay with
me until the end," broken by an instinctive movement, the
habit that made her respond to the lady in red, dragging
Howell to receive to his face the revealing words. Deprived
of the infinitesimal gap he would have needed to change the
direction those words definitely gave to what would come,
Rice saw the curtain fall. "Idiot," said the lady in red. "Get
out of here, Flora," the tall man ordered, sticking to Rice,
who smiled, satisfied. "Idiot," the lady in red repeated,
taking Eva by the arm (she had lowered her head and
seemed almost absent). A push showed Rice the way; he felt
perfectly happy. "Idiot," the tall man said in turn. The tug
at his head was almost brutal, but Rice took off the glasses
himself and handed them to the tall man. "The whisky
wasn't bad," he said. "If you want to give me the instructions for the last act . . ." Another shove almost threw him
on the ground and when he managed to straighten up,
slightly dizzy, they were already tripping along a poorly lit
gallery; the tall man had disappeared, and the other two
pressed against him, forcing him to keep moving with the
mere pressure of their bodies. There was a door with an
orange light above. "Change," said the man in grey handing
him his suit. Almost without giving him time to put on his
jacket, they opened the door with a kick; the push sent him
reeling out onto the sidewalk, the cold of an alley that
smelled of garbage. "Sons of bitches, I'll catch pneumonia,"
Rice thought, putting his hands in his pockets. There were
lights at the furthest end of the alley, from where the sound
of traffic came. On the first corner (they hadn't taken his

money or his papers) Rice recognized the entrance to the
theater. As nobody was preventing him from attending the
last act from his seat, he entered the warmth of the foyer,
the smoke and the talk of the people in the bar; he had time
for another whisky, but felt unable to think about anything.
A little before the curtain went up he managed to wonder
who would do Howell's role in the last act, and if another
poor sucker would be going through affabilities and threats
and eyeglasses; but the joke probably ended the same way
each night, because immediately he recognized the actor of
the first act, who read a letter in his study and silently
handed it to a pale Eva dressed in grey. "It's outrageous,"
Rice commented, turning to the person on his left. "How
can people stand for this changing of actors in the middle
of a play?" The man sighed wearily. "You never can tell with
these young authors today," he said. "Everything's a symbol,
I suppose." Rice settled comfortably in his seat, malignantly
savoring the murmur of the spectators, who didn't seem to
accept Howell's physical changes as passively as his neighbor. Nevertheless, the theatrical illusion took over almost
immediately, the actor was excellent, and the action hurried
along in such a way that it even surprised Rice, lost in a
pleasant indifference. The letter was Michael's, announcing
his departure from England; Eva read it and silently returned it; you could hear that she was crying with restraint.
Stay with me until the end, Eva had said. *Don't let them kill
me,* Eva had absurdly said. From the security of the stalls,
it was inconceivable that anything could happen to her on
that junk stage; the whole thing had been a continuous
swindle, a long hour of wigs and painted trees. Of course,
the predictable lady in red invaded the melancholic peace
of the study, where Howell's pardon and perhaps love could
be perceived in his silences, in his almost absentminded way
of tearing the letter and throwing it in the fire. It seemed

inevitable for the lady in red to insinuate that Michael's departure was a strategic move, and for Howell to make his scorn evident to her, which, however, would not preclude a polite invitation to tea. The servant's arrival with the tray vaguely amused Rice; tea seemed to be one of the playwright's principal recourses, especially now that the lady in red was fidgeting with a little bottle of romantic melodrama, while the lights faded in a completely unexplainable way in a London lawyer's chambers. There was a telephone call, which Howell answered with perfect composure (a fall in the stocks or any other necessary crisis was to be expected for the conclusion); the cups passed from hand to hand with the appropriate smiles, the proper tone before castastrophes. Howell's gesture the moment Eva brought the cup to her lips, his abrupt movement, and the tea spilling over her grey dress almost bothered Rice. Eva was motionless, almost ridiculous; in that instantaneous freeze of positions (Rice sat up straight without knowing why, and someone muttered impatiently behind him), the shocked exclamation of the lady in red drowned out the light cracking noise, Howell raised his hand to announce something, and Eva turned her head toward the audience, looking as if she refused to believe, and then slid sideways until almost lying on the sofa, in a slow renewal of movement which Howell seemed to receive and continue with his abrupt race toward the wings on the right, his flight which Rice didn't see, because he, too, was running up the center aisle before any other member of the audience had moved. Leaping down the stairs, he had the sense to hand in his check at the cloakroom and retrieve his coat; when he reached the door, he heard the first sounds of the play's end, applause, and voices in the hall; someone in the theater was running up stairs. He fled toward Kean Street and, as he passed the alley, seemed to see a bulk moving along the wall; the door they had thrown him out of was ajar, but Rice hadn't finished registering those images when he was running along the main street; instead of leaving the theater district he went down Kingsway again, not expecting anybody to think of looking for him near the theater. He reached the Strand (he had raised his coat collar and walked rapidly, with his hands in his pockets) until disappearing, with a relief he himself couldn't explain, into the vague region of small streets starting at Chancery Lane. Leaning against a wall (he panted a little and felt the sweat sticking his shirt to his skin), he lit a cigarette and for the first time explicitly asked himself, using all the necessary words, why he was fleeing. Approaching steps came between him and the answer he was looking for; while he ran, he thought that if he succeeded in crossing the river (he was already near Blackfriars Bridge), he would feel safe. He took refuge in a doorway, far from the street lamp that lighted the way toward Watergate. Something burned his mouth; he yanked out the forgotten butt, and felt it tearing his lips. In the silence surrounding him, he tried to repeat the unanswered questions, but was ironically interrupted by the idea that he would be safe only if he managed to cross the river. It was illogical; the footsteps, too, could follow him on the bridge, in any lane on the other bank; and still he chose the bridge, he ran with the wind in his favor, helping him to leave the river behind and disappear into a labyrinth he did not know until reaching a poorly lit area; the third pause of the night in a deep, narrow blind alley finally placed him before the only important question, and Rice realized that he couldn't find the answer. *Don't let them kill me*, Eva had said, and he had done all that was possible, awkwardly and miserably, but just the same they had killed her, at least in the play they had killed her, and he had to run away, because it couldn't be that the play ended like that, that the cup of tea spilled harmlessly over

Eva's dress, and yet Eva slid until she was lying on the sofa; something else had happened without his being there to prevent it. *Stay with me until the end,* Eva had begged him, but they had thrown him out of the theater, they had separated him from what had to happen and what he, stupidly settled in his seat, had contemplated without understanding, or understanding it from another region of himself where there was fear and flight and now, sticky like the sweat running down his belly, disgust in himself. "But I have nothing to do with it," he thought. "And nothing has happened; it isn't possible for things like that to happen." He repeated this to himself conscientiously: It couldn't be that they had come to get him, to propose that foolishness to him, to threaten him amiably; the footsteps that were coming closer had to be some vagabond's, footsteps without footprints. The redheaded man who stopped beside him almost without looking at him, and who took off his glasses with a convulsive gesture to put them on again after wiping them on the lapel of his jacket, was simply someone who looked like Howell, the actor who had played Howell's role and had spilled the cup of tea on Eva's dress. "Throw away that wig," Rice said. "They'll recognize you anywhere." "It's not a wig," said Howell. (His name must be Smith or Rogers, he didn't even remember the name on the program anymore) "What a fool I am!" said Rice. He could have guessed that they had prepared an exact copy of Howell's hair, just as the eyeglasses had been a replica of Howell's. "You did what you could," Rice said. "I was in the stalls and I saw it; everybody will be able to speak in your favor." Howell trembled, leaning against the wall. "It's not that," he said. "What does it matter, if they got their way anyhow?" Rice lowered his head; a great fatigue came over him. "I, too, tried to save her," he said, "but they wouldn't let me continue." Howell looked at him resentfully. "The same thing always happens," he said as if talking to himself. "That's typical of amateurs. They think they can do it better than the others, and in the end it's no use." He raised his collar, put his hands in his pockets. Rice would have liked to ask him: "Why does the same thing always happen? And if that's the case, why are we running away?" The sound of the whistle seemed engulfed in the lane, looking for them. They ran for a long time in a dead heat, until stopping on some corner smelling of oil, of stagnant river. Behind a pile of bales they rested a moment; Howell panted like a dog and Rice had a cramp in his calf. He rubbed it, leaning on the bales, standing with difficulty on one foot. "But perhaps it's not that serious," he murmured. "You said the same thing always happened." Howell put a hand over his mouth; the two whistles were alternating now. "Each go his own way," Howell said. "Maybe one of us can escape." Rice realized he was right, but he would have wanted Howell to answer him first. He took him by the arm, drawing him close with all his strength. "Don't let me go like this," he begged. "I can't keep running away forever, without knowing." He smelled the tarred odor of the bales; his hand felt sort of vacant in the air. Some footsteps were running away; Rice crouched, gathering impulse, and took off in the opposite direction. In the light of a street lamp he saw some name: Rose Alley. Further on was the river, some bridge. There would be no lack of bridges or streets on which to run.

ALL FIRES THE FIRE

THAT'S WHAT HIS STATUE will look like someday, the proconsul ironically thinks as he raises his arm, holds it in a formal salute, lets himself be petrified by a cheering crowd that two hours of circus and heat have not fatigued. It is the moment of the promised surprise; the proconsul lowers his arm, looks at his wife, who returns him the vacant smile of celebrations. Irene does not know what will follow and at the same time it's as if she knew, even the unexpected becomes habit when you have learned, with that indifference the proconsul hates, to put up with your master's whims. Without even turning toward the arena she foresees a die already cast, a cruel and monotonous succession of events. Licas the vineyard keeper and Urania his wife are the first to shout a name which the crowd picks up and repeats. "I was keeping this as a surprise for you," the proconsul says. "They've assured me that you admire the style of this gladiator." Guarding her smile as usual, Irene bows her head in thanks. "Since you do us the honor of joining us, even though the games bore you," the proconsul adds, "it's only right that I try to offer what pleases you most." "You are the salt of the earth!" Licas shouts. "You make the very shadow of Mars descend upon our poor provincial arena!" "You have seen only half of it," says the proconsul, wetting his lips on a goblet of wine and passing it to his wife. Irene takes a long sip, which seems to carry away with its light perfume the thick, persistent smell of blood and dung. In an abrupt silence of expectation that outlines him with relentless precision, Marcus moves toward the center of the arena; his short sword shines in the sun, there where one indirect ray passes through the old velarium, and the bronze shield hangs casually from his left hand. "Aren't you going to challenge him with Smirnio's victor?" Licas asks excitedly. "Better than that," the proconsul says. "I would like your province to remember me for these games, and my wife to cease to be bored." Urania and Licas applaud, waiting for Irene's reply, but she returns the goblet to the slave in silence, distant to the clamor greeting the second gladiator's arrival. Motionless, Marcus, too, seems indifferent to the cheers his adversary receives; with the tip of his sword, he lightly touches his golden greaves.

"Hello," says Roland Renoir, choosing a cigarette like an unavoidable continuation of the act of picking up the receiver. On the line there's a crackling of mixed communications, someone dictating figures, suddenly a silence still darker than that darkness the telephone pours into the eye of his ear. "Hello," Roland repeats, resting his cigarette on the edge of the ashtray and looking for his matches in the pocket of his bathrobe. "It's me," says Jeanne's voice. Roland, weary, half closes his eyes and stretches out in a more comfortable position. "It's me," Jeanne repeats uselessly. As Roland doesn't answer, she adds: "Sonia has just left."

His duty is to look toward the imperial box, to make the

usual salute. He knows that he must do it and that he will
see the proconsul's wife and the proconsul, and that perhaps
she will smile to him as in the last games. He doesn't need
to think, he almost doesn't know how to think, but instinct
tells him that this arena is bad, the enormous bronze eye
where hoes and palm leaves have sketched their curved
paths darkened by traces of preceding fights. That night he
dreamed of a fish, he dreamed of a lonely road between
broken columns; while he dressed, someone murmured that
the proconsul will not pay him in gold coins. Marcus did not
bother to ask, and the other laughed perversely before walking away without turning his back to him; a third man,
afterwards, told him that he was a brother of a gladiator
Marcus had killed in Massilia, but they were already pushing
him toward the gallery, toward the shouting outside. The
heat is unbearable, his helmet, returning the sun's rays to the
velarium and the stands, feels heavy. A fish, broken columns;
dreams without clear meaning, with forgotten moments
that keep him from understanding. And the one who
dressed him said that the proconsul will not pay him in gold
coins; perhaps the proconsul's wife would not smile at him
this afternoon. The cheering leaves him unmoved, because
now they're applauding the other one, they applaud him less
than they did Marcus a moment ago, but through the applause come shouts of astonishment, and Marcus raises his
head, looks toward the box, where Irene has turned to speak
to Urania, where the proconsul is casually making a signal,
and his whole body stiffens, and his hand closes tightly
around the hilt of his sword. It was enough for him to turn
his eyes toward the opposite gallery. It is not through there
that his rival appears; they have raised the creaking gates of
the dark passage where they have the wild animals come out,
and Marcus sees the gigantic figure of the Nubian retiarius
appear, until then invisible against the background of mossy

stone; now he knows beyond all doubt that the proconsul will not pay him in gold coins, he guesses the meaning of the fish and the broken columns. And at the same time, it hardly matters to him what will happen with the retiarius —that's part of his job and fate—but his body is still tight as if he were afraid, something in his flesh wonders why the retiarius has come out through the animals' gallery, and the crowd also wonders about it between cheers, and Licas asks the proconsul, who smiles to underline the surprise without a word, and Licas protests laughing and feels compelled to bet on Marcus; before hearing the words that will follow, Irene knows that the proconsul will double his bet on the Nubian, and that, after, he will look at her amiably and order chilled wine, and she will drink the wine and comment to Urania on the Nubian's height and ferocity. Each motion is predicted, although one doesn't notice it, although the goblet of wine or the gesture of Urania's mouth while she admires the giant's body be missing. Then Licas, expert in countless circus events, will have them notice that the Nubian's helmet has brushed the barbs of the animals' gate, two yards and six inches above the ground, and he will praise the ease with which he arranges the scales of the net over his left arm. As usual, as from a now distant wedding night, Irene falls back on the deepest boundary of herself while on the outside she complies and smiles and even enjoys; in that free and sterile deep she feels the sign of death that the proconsul has concealed in a happy public surprise, the sign that only she and perhaps Marcus can understand, but Marcus, grim, silent, machine, will not understand, and his body that she desired on another circus afternoon (which the proconsul has guessed, without his magicians' aid, he has guessed it as usual, from the first moment) will pay the price of mere imagination, of a double futile look upon the corpse of a Thracian skillfully killed by a gash in the throat.

Before dialing Roland's number, Jeanne's hand wandered through the pages of a fashion magazine, over a tube of tranquilizers, the back of her cat curled up on the sofa. Then Roland's voice said: "Hello," a bit sleepy, and suddenly Jeanne has had a sensation of ridicule, that she's going to say to Roland what precisely will put her into the gallery of telephonic weepers, with the one ironic spectator smoking in condescending silence. "It's me," Jeanne says, but more for herself than to that silence on the other side in which, like background, some sparks of sound dance. She looks at her hand, which has absently petted the cat before dialing the numbers (and can't other numbers be heard on the telephone, isn't there a distant voice that dictates figures to someone who doesn't speak, who is there only to copy obediently?), refusing to believe that the hand which has raised and put the tube of pills down again is her hand, that the voice which has just repeated: "It's me" is her voice, at the edge of the boundary. For dignity, keep quiet, slowly return the receiver to its hook, remain cleanly alone. "Sonia has just left," Jeanne says, and the boundary is crossed, the ridiculous begins, the little comfortable hell.

"Oh," Roland says, striking a match. Jeanne distinctly hears the match, it's as if she saw Roland's face as he inhales the smoke, leaning back a little with his eyes half-closed. A river of shining scales seems to jump out of the black giant's hand, and Marcus is just in time to dodge the net. Other times—the proconsul knows it and turns his head so that only Irene will see him smile—he has taken advantage of that short second, which is the weak point of every retiarius, to block the threat of the long trident with his shield and thrust with a flashing motion toward the uncovered chest. But Marcus keeps himself out of range, his legs bent as if to jump, while the Nubian rapidly picks up the net and prepares the new attack. "He's lost," Irene thinks without looking at the proconsul, who picks some sweets off the tray Urania offers him. "He's not the same," Licas thinks, regretting his bet. Marcus has bent over a little, following the Nubian's circling motion; he's the only one who still doesn't know what everyone forebodes; he's barely something which, crouched, awaits another opportunity, with the vague confusion of not having done what his science commanded. He would need more time, the tavern hours which follow triumphs, to perhaps understand why the proconsul is not going to pay him in gold coins. Sullen, he waits for another propitious moment; maybe at the end, with a foot upon the retiarius' corpse, he can again find the smile of the proconsul's wife; but he's not thinking that, and the one who is thinking it no longer believes that Marcus' foot will kneel on the chest of a slain Nubian.

"Make up your mind," Roland says, "unless you want to keep me listening the whole afternoon to that guy who's dictating numbers to God knows who. Can you hear him?" "Yes," Jeanne says. "He sounds very far away. Three hundred and sixty-four, two hundred and forty-two." For a moment there's only the distant, monotonous voice. "In any case," Roland says, "he's using the phone for something practical." The answer could have been predictable, the first complaint, but Jeanne keeps still a few seconds more and repeats: "Sonia has just left." She hesitates before adding: "She'll probably arrive at your house any moment now." That would surprise Roland, there's no reason for Sonia to go to his house. "Don't lie," Jeanne says, and the cat runs from her hand, looks at her offended. "It wasn't a lie," Roland says. "I was referring to the time, not to the fact of her coming or not coming. Sonia knows that visits and calls at this hour bother me." Eight hundred and five, the voice dictates far away. Four hundred and sixteen. Thirty-two. Jeanne has closed her eyes, waiting for the first pause in that anonymous voice to say the only thing that's left to say. If Roland hangs up, that voice in the background will still be left, she'll be able to keep the receiver to her ear, slipping further and further down on the sofa, caressing the cat who has come to lie against her again, playing with the tube of pills, listening to the figures until the other voice will also tire, and nothing will be left, absolutely nothing except the receiver, which will begin to weigh frightfully between her fingers, a dead thing she'll have to reject without looking at it. One hundred and forty-five, says the voice. And still further away, like a tiny sketch in pencil, someone who could be a shy woman asks between two crackles: "The North station?"

For the second time, he manages to get clear of the net, but he has miscalculated the jump and slips on a damp spot in the sand. With an effort that makes the crowd stand up, Marcus rejects the net with a swing of his sword, while he extends his left arm and receives the resonant blow of the trident on his shield. The proconsul scorns Licas' excited remarks and turns his head toward Irene, who hasn't moved. "Now or never," the proconsul says. "Never," Irene answers. "He's not the same," Licas repeats, "and it's going to cost him dearly, the Nubian's not going to give him another chance, just look at him." At a distance, almost motionless, Marcus seems to have realized his error; with the shield up high he stares at the already gathered net, the trident that sways hypnotically two yards from his eyes. "You're right, he's not the same man," the proconsul says. "Did you bet on him, Irene?" Crouching, ready to jump, Marcus feels on his skin, in the pit of his stomach, that the crowd is abandoning him. If he had a moment of calm, he could break the knot that paralyzes him, the invisible chain that begins way back, who knows where, and that in some moment is the proconsul's request, the promise of an extraordinary pay-

ment, and also a dream where there's a fish, and also feeling
now when there's no longer time for anything, the very
image of the dream facing the net that dances before his
eyes and seems to catch every ray of sun that filters through
the holes in the velarium. Everything is a chain, a trap;
standing straight with a threatening violence that the audience applauds, while the retiarius steps back for the first
time, Marcus chooses the only way, confusion and sweat and
the smell of blood, the death before him that he must crush;
someone is thinking it for him behind the smiling mask,
someone has desired it over the body of a dying Thracian.
"Poison," Irene thinks, "someday I will find the poison, but
now accept the wine from him, be the stronger one, wait
your time." The pause seems to extend as the insidious black
gallery, where the faraway voice which repeats figures and
returns intermittently, extends. Jeanne has always believed
that the messages which really count are at some point
beyond all words; perhaps those figures say more, are more
than any speech for the one who's attentively listening to
them, as Sonia's perfume was for her; the brushing of the
palm of her hand on her shoulder before leaving were so
much more than Sonia's words. But it was natural for Sonia
not to be satisfied with a ciphered message, that she wanted
to spell it out, relishing it till the last. "I know it will be very
hard for you," Sonia has repeated, "but I hate pretending,
I prefer to tell you the truth." Five hundred and forty-six,
six hundred and seventy-two, two hundred and eighty-nine.
"I don't care if she goes to see you or not," Jeanne says. "I
don't care about anything now." Instead of another figure,
there's a long silence. "Are you still there?" Jeanne asks.
"Yes," Roland says, leaving the butt in the ashtray and
calmly reaching for the flask of cognac. "What I can't understand . . .," Jeanne begins. "Please," Roland says, "in
these cases, nobody understands much of anything, dear,

and besides you don't gain anything by understanding. I'm sorry Sonia has rushed it, it wasn't for her to tell you. God-damn it, isn't he ever going to finish with those numbers?" The small voice, which makes one think of a world of ants, continues its precise dictation underneath a nearer and thicker silence. "But you," Jeanne says absurdly, "then, you . . ."

Roland takes a sip of cognac. He has always liked to choose his words, to avoid superfluous dialogues. Jeanne will repeat each sentence twice, three times, accenting them differently each time; let her talk, let her repeat while he thinks up the basic and sensible answers that will impose some order upon her deplorable fit. Breathing hard, he straightens up after a thrust and side advance; something tells him that this time the Nubian is going to change the order of the attack, that the trident will be thrust before the net. "Watch carefully," Licas explains to his wife. "I've seen him do it at Apta Iulia, it always confuses them." Poorly defended, defying the risk of entering the net's field, Marcus lunges forward and only then raises the shield to protect himself from the shining river that escapes the Nubian's hand like lightning. He intercepts the edge of the net but the trident strikes low, and blood leaps from Marcus' thigh, while the sword, too short, resounds futilely against its shaft. "I told you so," Licas shouts. The proconsul looks atten-tively at the lacerated thigh, the blood it loses into the golden greave; he thinks, almost feeling pity, that Irene would have liked to caress that thigh, seek its pressure and warmth, moaning as she knows how when he draws her close to hurt her. He'll say this tonight, and it will be interesting to study Irene's face, looking for the weak spot in her perfect mask, which will fake indifference till the end, as it now fakes a polite interest in the fight, which makes a mob, suddenly excited by the approaching end, howl with enthu-

siasm. "Luck has abandoned him," the proconsul says to
Irene. "I almost feel guilty for having brought him here to
this provincial arena; a part of him has stayed in Rome,
that's clear to see." "And the rest will stay here, with the
money I bet on him," Licas laughs. "Please, don't get like
that," Roland says. "It's absurd to keep talking on the phone
when we can see each other tonight. I'll say it again, Sonia
has rushed things, I wanted to spare you that blow." The ant
has stopped dictating numbers, and Jeanne's voice can be
heard distinctly; there are no tears in her voice, which surprises Roland, who has prepared his words with an avalanche
of accusations in mind. "Spare me the blow?" Jeanne says.
"Lying, naturally, deceiving me one more time." Roland
sighs, dismissing the answers that could draw out a tedious
dialogue indefinitely. "I'm sorry, but if you keep on like that,
I'd rather hang up," he says, and for the first time there's
a friendly tone in his voice. "It would be better for me to
come and see you tomorrow. After all, we are civilized people, damn it." Very far away the ant dictates: eight hundred
and eighty-eight. "Don't come," Jeanne says, and it's fun to
hear the words mixing with the numbers, don't eight
hundred come and eighty-eight, "don't come any more,
Roland." Melodrama, the probable suicide threats, the bore-
dom of it, the way it happened with Marie Josée, the way
it happens when all of them take it so tragically. "Don't be
silly," Roland advises. "You'll understand it better tomorrow, it's better for both of us." Jeanne is silent, the ant
dictates round numbers: one hundred, four hundred, one
thousand. "Well, see you tomorrow," Roland says, admiring
the clothes on Sonia, who's just opened the door and is
standing there with a half-questioning, half-mocking look.
"She didn't lose any time in calling you," Sonia says, putting
down her pocketbook and a magazine. "See you tomorrow,
Jeanne," Roland repeats. The silence on the line seems to

stretch like a bow, until a distant number, nine hundred and four, cuts into it. "Stop dictating those stupid numbers!" Roland shouts at the top of his voice, and before putting the receiver down he manages to hear the click on the other end, the bow that lets go of its harmless arrow. Paralyzed, knowing he's unable to avoid the net that will soon surround him, Marcus faces the Nubian giant, his much too short sword at the end of his arm. The Nubian slackens the net once, twice, gathers it up, looking for the most favorable position, still swings it around, as if he wanted to keep the crowd, which incites him to finish off his rival, howling, and then he lowers the trident while he moves to one side to give the thrust more impulse. Marcus goes to meet the net with his shield up high, and he is a tower that crumbles against a black mass, his sword sinks into something that howls further up; sand gets into his mouth and eyes, the net falls uselessly over the fish that drowns.

He accepts the caresses indifferently, unable to feel that Jeanne's hand trembles a little and begins to grow cold. When the fingers slide down his fur and stop, planted in a sudden contraction, the cat growls petulantly; then he rolls over on his back and moves his paws in the expectant position that always makes Jeanne laugh, but not now. Her hand remains motionless beside the cat, and only one finger still seeks the warmth of his fur, moving briefly over it before stopping again between the warm flank and the tube of pills that has rolled there. Pierced in the stomach, the Nubian howls, falling back a step, and in that last moment, when pain is like a flame of hate, all the strength that flees his body rushes to his arm to sink the trident into the back of his rival lying face down. He falls on Marcus' body, and convulsions make him roll to one side; Marcus slowly moves his arm, pinned to the arena like an enormous shining insect.

"It is not frequent," the proconsul says, turning to

Irene, "that two gladiators of such worth kill each other. We can congratulate ourselves on having seen a rare spectacle. Tonight I will write to my brother about it to console him in his tedious marriage."

Irene sees Marcus' arm move, a slow futile movement, as if he wanted to pull the trident out of his kidneys. She imagines the proconsul naked in the arena, with the same trident nailed into him to the shaft. But the proconsul would not move his arm with that last dignity; he would scream and kick like a hare, he would beg the indignant crowd's pardon. Accepting the hand her husband offers to help her rise, she assents once more; the arm has stopped moving, the only thing left to do is smile, take refuge in intelligence. The cat doesn't seem to like Jeanne's stillness, he remains on his back waiting for a caress; then, as if that finger against his fur bothered him, he meows ill-humoredly and turns over to walk away, already forgetful and sleepy.

"Forgive me for coming at this hour," Sonia says, "I saw your car at the door, the temptation was too great. She called you, right?" Roland looks for a cigarette. "You did the wrong thing," he says. "That's supposed to be the man's job. After all, I've been with Jeanne for more than two years, and she's a nice girl." "Oh, but the fun of it," Sonia says, pouring herself some cognac. "I've never been able to forgive her for being so innocent, it's the most exasperating thing. Just imagine, she laughed at first, she thought I was kidding." Roland looks at the telephone, thinks of the ant. Now Jeanne will call again, and it will be uncomfortable, because Sonia has sat next to him and is caressing his hair while she leafs through a literary magazine as if she were looking for pictures. "You did the wrong thing," Roland repeats, drawing Sonia to him. "In coming at this hour?" Sonia laughs, yielding to the hands that awkwardly seek the first zipper. The purple veil covers Irene's shoulders as she turns her back on the crowd, waiting for the proconsul to salute for the last time. The cheers are already mixed with a sound of people in motion, the hurried race to get out and reach the lower galleries first. Irene knows the slaves will be dragging the corpses away and she doesn't turn around; it pleases her to know that the proconsul has accepted Licas' invitation to dine in his villa on the shores of the lake, where the night air will help her forget the smell of the mob, the last shouts, an arm moving slowly as if it caressed the earth. It's not hard for her to forget, although the proconsul harasses her with the detailed evocation of the past that disturbs him; one day, Irene will find the way of making him forget forever, too, and so that people will simply think he's dead. "You'll see what our cook has invented," Licas' wife is saying. "He's brought my husband's appetite back, and at night . . ." Licas laughs and greets his friends, waiting for the proconsul to begin the procession toward the gallery after a last salute which is slow in coming, as if it pleased him to keep looking at the arena, where they hook up and drag away the corpses. "I'm so happy," Sonia says, leaning her cheek against Roland's chest. "Don't say it," Roland drowsily murmurs. "One always thinks that's a kindness." "Don't you believe me?" Sonia laughs. "Yes, but don't say it now. Let's just smoke." He gropes on the low table until he finds cigarettes, he puts one between Sonia's lips, brings his own near, lights them both at the same time. Sleepy, they hardly look at each other, and Roland shakes the match and puts it on the table, where there's an ashtray somewhere. Sonia is the first to doze off, and he very gently takes the cigarette out of her mouth, puts it together with his and leaves them on the table, sliding against Sonia in a heavy and imageless sleep. The gauze kerchief burns without flame on the edge of the ashtray; scorching slowly, it falls on the rug next to the pile of clothes and a glass of cognac. Part of the crowd shouts and piles together on the lower stands; the proconsul has saluted once more and makes a signal to his guards to clear the way. Licas, the first to understand, points to the furthest canvas of the old velarium, which is beginning to tear, while a rain of sparks falls over the people seeking exits in confusion. Shouting an order, the proconsul pushes Irene, always with her back turned and motionless. "Hurry, before they crowd into the lower gallery," Licas shouts hurrying before his wife. Irene is the first to smell the boiling oil, the burning of the underground deposits; behind her, the velarium falls on the backs of those who struggle to get through the mass of confused bodies that obstruct the too narrow galleries. People jump to the arena by the hundreds, seeking other exits, but the smoke of the oil erases images, a shred of material floats on the tip of the flames and falls on the proconsul before he can take shelter in the passage that leads to the imperial gallery. Irene turns upon hearing his scream, picks the scorched cloth off him with two fingers, delicately. "We won't be able to get out," she says. "They're heaped together down there like animals." Sonia screams, trying to break loose from the burning arm that surrounds her from sleep, and her first scream joins with Roland's, who tries in vain to sit up straight, stifled by the black smoke. They are still screaming, more and more faintly, when the fire engine rushes full speed into the street crammed with the curious. "It's on the tenth floor," the lieutenant says. "It's going to be hard, there's a wind from the north. Let's go."

THE OTHER HEAVEN

Ces yeux ne t'appartiennent
pas . . . où les as-tu pris?
. . . ., IV, 5.

IT WOULD SOMETIMES occur to me that everything would let
go, soften, give in, accepting without resistance that you can
move like that from one thing to another. I'm saying that
this would occur to me, although a stupid hope would like
to believe that it might yet occur to me. And that's why, if
strolling around the city time and again seems shocking
when you have a family and a job, there are times when I
keep repeating to myself that there would be time to return
to my favorite neighborhood, forget about my work (I'm a
stockbroker), and with a little luck find Josiane and stay with
her till the next morning.

Who knows how long I've been repeating all this to
myself? And it's pitiful, because there was a time when
things happened to me when I least thought of them, barely
pushing with my shoulder any corner of the air. In any case,
it would be enough to become one of those citizens who let
themselves get pleasurably carried away by their favorite

streets, and almost always my walk ended in the gallery district, perhaps because arcades and galleries have always been my secret country. Here, for example, the Güemes Arcade, an ambiguous territory where, so many years ago, I went to strip off my childhood like a used suit. Around the year 1928, the Güemes Arcade was the treasure cave in which a glimpse of sin and mint drops deliciously mixed, where they cried out the evening editions with crimes on every page, and the lights burned in the basement movie theater where they showed restricted blue movies. The Josianes of those days must have looked at me with faces both maternal and amused, I with a few miserable cents in my pocket, but walking like a man, my hat slouched and my hands in my pockets, smoking a *Commander*, precisely because my stepfather had predicted that I would end up blind from foreign cigarettes. I especially remember smells and sounds, something like an expectation and an anxiety, the stand where you could buy magazines with naked women and advertisements of false manicures; already then I was sensitive to that false sky of dirty stucco and skylights, to that artificial night which ignored the stupidity of day and the sun outside. With false indifference, I'd peek into the doors of the arcade where the last mystery began, the vague elevators that would lead to the offices of VD doctors and also to the presumed paradises higher up, of women of the town and perverts, as they would call them in the newspapers, with preferably green drinks in cut glass goblets, with silk gowns and violet kimonos, and the apartments would have the same perfume that came out of the stores, which I thought were so elegant and which sparked an unreachable bazaar of bottles and glass boxes and pink and rachel powder puffs and brushes with transparent handles over the low light of the arcade.

It's still hard for me to cross the Güemes Arcade without feeling ironically tender toward that memory of adolescence at the brink of the fall; the old fascination still persists, and that's why I liked to walk without a fixed destination, knowing that at any moment I would enter the region of the galleries, where any sordid, dusty shop would attract me more than the show windows facing the insolence of the open streets. The Galerie Vivienne, for example, or the Passage des Panoramas with its branches, its short cuts which end in a secondhand book shop or a puzzling travel agency, where perhaps nobody ever even bought a railroad ticket, that world which has chosen a nearer sky, of dirty windows and stucco with allegorical figures that extend their hands to offer garlands, that Galerie Vivienne one step from the daily shame of the Rue Réaumur and of the Bourse (I work at the stock exchange), how much of that district has always been mine, even before I suspected it was already mine when posted on a corner of the Güemes Arcade, counting the few cents I had as a student, I would argue the problem of spending them in an automat or buying a novel and a supply of sour balls in their cellophane bag, with a cigarette that clouded my eyes and, in the bottom of my pocket where my fingers would sometimes rub against it, the little envelope with the rubber bought with false boldness at a drugstore run only by men, and which I would not have the least opportunity of using with so little money and such a childish face?

My fiancée, Irma, cannot understand what I like about wandering around at night downtown or in the southside district, and if she knew how I liked the Güemes Arcade she would not fail to be shocked. For her, as for my mother, there is no better social treat than the drawing room sofa, where what they call conversation, coffee, and the after-dinner liqueur take place. Irma is the kindest and most generous of women. I would never dream of talking to her

about the things that count most for me, and in that way
I will at some point be a good husband and a father, whose
sons will also be the much desired grandsons of my mother.
I suppose it was because of things like this that I ended up
meeting Josiane, but not only for that, since I could have
met her on the Boulevard Poissonnière or on the Rue Notre-
Dame-des-Victoires, and instead we looked at each other for
the first time in deepest Galerie Vivienne, under the plaster
figures which the gaslight would fill with trembling (the
garlands moved back and forth between the fingers of the
dusty muses), and it didn't take long to know that Josiane
worked in that district and that it wouldn't be difficult to
find her if you were acquainted with the cafés or friendly
with the coach drivers. It might have been a coincidence,
but having known her there, while it rained in the other
world, that of the high garlandless sky of the street, seemed
like a sign that went beyond the trivial meeting with any
prostitute of the district. Afterwards, I learned that, in those
days, Josiane never left the gallery, because it was the time
when all they talked about were the crimes of Laurent, and
the poor thing lived in fear. Some of that terror turned into
graceful, almost evasive, gestures, pure desire. I remember
her half-greedy, half-suspicious way of looking at me, her
questions which faked indifference, my almost unbelieving
fascination at finding out that she lived in the heights of the
gallery, my insistence upon going up to her garret instead of
going to the Rue du Sentier hotel (where she had friends and
felt protected). And her trust later on—how we laughed that
night at the very idea that I could be Laurent, and how
pretty and sweet Josiane was in her dime-novel garret, with
her fear of the strangler roaming around Paris and that way
of pressing closer to me as we reviewed the murders of
Laurent.

My mother always knows if I haven't slept at home,

and although she naturally doesn't say anything, since it would be absurd for her to do so, for one or two days she looks at once offendedly and fearfully at me. I know very well that she'd never think of telling Irma, but just the same the persistence of a maternal right, which is not at all justified now, annoys me, and especially since I will be the one who in the end comes back with a box of candy or a plant for the patio, and since the gift will represent in a very precise and taken-for-granted way the end of the offense, the return to everyday life of the son who still lives in his mother's house. Josiane was, of course, happy when I'd tell her about those episodes, which, once in the gallery district, would become part of our world with the same plainness of their protagonist. Josiane had great feeling for family life and she was full of respect for institutions and relatives; I'm not big on secrets, but since we had to talk about something and what she had revealed about her life had already been discussed, we would almost inevitably return to my problems as a single man. We had something else in common, and in that, too, I was lucky, since Josiane liked the galleries, perhaps because she lived in one, or because they protected her from cold and rain. (I met her early one winter, with premature snows our galleries and their world gaily ignored.) We got into the habit of taking walks when she had time, when someone—she didn't like to call him by his name—was content enough to let her enjoy herself with her friends for a while. We spoke little of that someone, after I had asked the inevitable questions, and she told the inevitable lies of all mercenary relationships; you took for granted that she was the boss, but he had the good taste not to make himself visible. I got to thinking it didn't annoy him when I kept Josiane company some nights. The Laurent threat lay heavier than ever upon the district after his new crime on the Rue d'Aboukir, and the poor thing wouldn't have dared to stray from the Galerie Vivienne once night had fallen. It was enough to make one feel grateful to Laurent and the boss; someone else's fears helped me do the rounds of the arcades and cafés with Josiane, discovering that I could be a real friend to a girl with whom I had no deep relationship. We gradually began to realize, through silences, foolish things about that trusted friendship. Her room, for example, the clean little garret that for me had no other reality than being part of the gallery. In the beginning I had gone up for Josiane, and as I couldn't stay because I didn't have the money to pay for a whole night, and someone was waiting for a spotless rendition of accounts, I almost couldn't see what was around me, and much later, when I was about to fall asleep in my shabby room with its illustrated calendar and silver maté gourd as its only luxuries, I wondered about the garret, but couldn't picture it. I saw only Josiane, and that was enough to put me to sleep, as if I still held her in my arms. But with friendship came prerogatives, perhaps the boss's consent, and Josiane managed it many times so that I could spend the night with her, and her room began to fill the gaps of our dialogue, which wasn't always easy; each doll, each picture card, each ornament settled in my memory and helped me to live when it was time to go back to my room or to talk with my mother or Irma about the nation's politics or family sicknesses.

Later there were other things, and among them the vague figure of the one Josiane called the South American, but in the beginning everything seemed centered around the great terror of the district, nourished by what an imaginative newspaperman had called the saga of Laurent the strangler. If, in a given moment, I conjure up the image of Josiane, it is to see her enter the Rue des Jeûneurs café with me, settle down on the purple felt bench, and exchange greetings with friends and regular customers, scattered

words which immediately are Laurent, because down by the
stock exchange all one talks about is Laurent, and I who have
worked the whole day on end, who, between two sessions of
quotations, have had to put up with the comments of col-
leagues and customers on Laurent's latest crime, wonder if
that stupid nightmare will end someday, if things will go
back to being as I imagine they were before Laurent, or if
we will have to suffer his macabre amusements until the end
of time. And the most irritating thing (I say to Josiane after
ordering the grog we so much need after that cold and snow)
is that we don't even know his name. They call him Laurent
because a clairvoyant of the Clichy neighborhood has seen
in her crystal ball how the murderer wrote his name with a
bloody finger, and the newspapermen are careful not to go
against the public's instinct. Josiane is no fool, but nobody
could convince her that the murderer's name is not Laurent,
and it's useless to fight against the eager terror fluttering in
her blue eyes, which are now absently looking at a very tall
and slightly stoop-shouldered young man, who has just come
in and is leaning on the counter and not greeting anyone.

"It's possible," Josiane says, accepting some soothing
thought that I must have invented without even thinking.
"But meanwhile I have to go up to my room alone, and if
the wind blows out the candle between floors . . . The very
idea of getting stuck on the stairs in the dark, and that
maybe . . ."

"You don't go up alone very often," I laugh.

"You can laugh, but there are bad nights, precisely
when it's snowing or raining, and I have to come back at two
in the morning . . ."

She continues her description of Laurent crouching on
a landing, or still worse, waiting for her in her room which
he has gotten into by means of a skeleton key. At the next
table Kiki shivers bombastically and lets out little screams

which multiply in the mirrors. We, the men, get a big kick out of these theatrical frights, which will help us protect our companions more prestigiously. It's a pleasure to smoke pipes in the café, at that hour when alcohol and tobacco begin to erase the fatigue of work, and the women compare their hats and boas or laugh at nothing; it's a pleasure to kiss Josiane, who has become so pensive looking at the man— almost a boy—whose back is turned to us, and who drinks his absinthe in little sips, leaning his elbow on the counter. It's curious, now that I think of it: with the first image of Josiane that comes to my mind, which is always Josiane on the café bench, a snowy, Laurent night, inevitably comes the one she called the South American, drinking his absinthe with his back to us. I called him the South American, too, because Josiane assured me that he was, and that she knew this through La Rousse, who had gone to bed with him or just about, and all that had happened before Josiane and La Rousse had a fight over corners or hours, which they now regretted with halfway words, because they had been very good friends. According to La Rousse, he had told her that he was South American, although he spoke without the slightest accent; he had told her that before going to bed with her, perhaps to make small talk while he finished untying his shoes.

"It's hard to believe, him almost a boy . . . Doesn't he look like a schoolboy who's suddenly grown up? Well, you should hear what La Rousse says."

Josiane persisted in her habit of crossing and uncrossing her fingers every time she told an exciting story. She explained the South American's whim to me, nothing so extraordinary after all, La Rousse's flat refusal, the customer's self-possessed exit. I asked her if the South American had ever approached her. Well no, because he probably knew that La Rousse and she were friends. He knew them well, he lived in the neighborhood, and when Josiane said that, I looked more carefully and saw him pay for his absinthe, throwing a coin into the little pewter dish while he slid over us—and it was as if we ceased to be there for an endless second—a both distant and curiously fixed expression, the face of someone who has immobilized himself in a moment of his dream and refuses to take the step that will return him to wakefulness. After all, an expression like that, although the boy was almost an adolescent and had very beautiful features, could easily lead one back to the recurrent nightmare of Laurent. I didn't lose a minute in suggesting this to Josiane.

"Laurent? Are you crazy? Why Laurent is . . ."

The thing is nobody knew anything about Laurent, although Kiki and Albert helped us to keep weighing the possibilities to amuse ourselves. The whole theory fell to pieces when the café owner, who miraculously heard everything that was said in the café, reminded us that at least one thing was known about Laurent: the great strength that enabled him to strangle his victims with one hand only. And that boy, come on . . . Yes, and it was late already and a good time to go home; I would be alone that night, because Josiane would spend it with someone who was already waiting for her in the garret, someone who had the key because he had the right to, and I accompanied her to the first landing so that she wouldn't get scared if the candle went out while she was walking up, and with a sudden great fatigue I watched her go, perhaps happy, although she would have said the opposite, and then I went out into the snowy, icy street and started walking in any direction, until at one point I found as always the road that would take me back to my neighborhood, among people who read the late-night edition of the newspapers or looked out of the trolleycar windows, as if there really was something to see at that hour and on those streets.

It wasn't always easy to get to the gallery district at the moment Josiane was free; so many times I had to wander alone through the arcades, a bit disappointed, until I began to feel that night, too, was my mistress. The moment they turned on the gaslights, things would come alive in our kingdom; the cafés were the stock exchange of idleness and content, you'd drink in the end of the day, the headlines, politics, the Prussians, Laurent, the horse races, in long gulps. I enjoyed having a drink here and another further on, leisurely watching for the moment when I'd spy Josiane's figure in some corner of the galleries or at some bar. If she already had company, a chosen signal would let me know when I could find her alone; other times she simply smiled, and I was left to devote my time to the galleries; those were the explorer's hours, and so I ventured into the farthest regions of the neighborhood, the Galerie Sainte-Foy, for example, and the remote Passage du Caire, but even though any of them attracted me more than the open streets (and there were so many—today it was the Passage des Princes, another time the Passage Verdeau, and so on to infinity), the end of a long tour which I myself wouldn't have been able to reconstruct always took me back to the Galerie Vivienne, not so much because of Josiane, although also for her, but for its protective gates, its ancient allegories, its shadows in the corner of the Passage des Petits-Pères, that different world where you didn't have to think about Irma and could live not by regular schedules, but by chance encounters and luck. With so little to hang on to, I can't calculate the time that passed before we casually talked about the South American again; once I thought I saw him coming out of a doorway on the Rue Saint-Marc, wrapped in one of those black student gowns they'd been wearing so much five years back, together with excessively tall top hats, and I was tempted to go and ask him about his origins. The thought of the cold anger with which I would have received an inquiry of that sort prevented me, but Josiane later considered that this had been foolish on my part, perhaps because the South American interested her in her own way, with something of professional offense and a lot of curiosity. She remembered that some nights back she thought she recognized him at a distance in the Galerie Vivienne, which he didn't seem to frequent, however.

"I don't like the way he looks at us," said Josiane. "Before it didn't matter, but ever since that time you talked about Laurent . . ."

"Josiane, when I made that joke we were with Kiki and Albert. Albert is a police informer, as you must know. You think he would let the opportunity go if the idea seemed reasonable to him? Laurent's head is worth a lot of money, dear."

"I don't like his eyes," Josiane insisted. "And besides, he doesn't look at people. He stares, but he doesn't look at you. If he ever comes over to me I'll run like the dickens, I swear to God."

"You're afraid of a boy. Or are all us South Americans orangutans to you?"

You can already imagine how those dialogues would end. We'd go and have a grog at the café on the Rue des Jeûneurs, we'd wander around the galleries, the theaters on the boulevard, we'd go up to the garret, we'd have a great laugh. There were several weeks—it's so hard to be precise with happiness—when everything made us laugh. Even Badinguet's clumsiness and the fear of the war amused us. It's almost ridiculous to admit that something as disproportionately base as Laurent could crush our happiness, but that's how it was. Laurent killed another woman on the Rue Beauregard—so close, after all—and in the café it was like being at Mass, and Marthe, who had come racing in shouting the news ended in an explosion of hysterical tears which somehow helped us swallow the knot in our throats. That same night the police went through all of us with its finest comb, in every café and every hotel; Josiane went to her boss, and I let her go, knowing that she needed the supreme protection that smoothed away all cares. But since basically that kind of thing made me vaguely sad—the galleries weren't meant for that, shouldn't be for that—I began drinking with Kiki and then with La Rousse, who sought me out as the bridge she needed to make up with Josiane. People drank heartily at our café, and in that hot mist of voices and drink it seemed almost perfect that at midnight the South American sat at a table in the back and ordered his absinthe with that same beautiful and absent and moon-struck expression. At La Rousse's first intimation, I told her that I already knew, and that, after all, the boy wasn't blind and his tastes did not deserve such resentment; we even laughed at La Rousse's make-believe punches when Kiki deigned to say that once she had been in his room. Before La Rousse could claw her with a predictable question, I wanted to know what that room was like. "Bah, what does the room matter?" La Rousse said disdainfully, but Kiki was already plunging into a garret on the Rue Notre-Dame-des-Victoires and, like a bad small-town magician, pulling out a gray cat, piles of scribbled papers, a piano which took up too much room, but above all papers, and finally the gray cat again, which, deep down, seemed to be Kiki's favorite memory.

I let her talk, looking all the time toward the table in the back and thinking that after all it would have been so natural to go over to the South American and say a few words to him in Spanish. I was about to do it, and now I'm only one of many who wonder why at some point they didn't do what they felt like doing. Instead, I remained with La Rousse and Kiki, smoking a new pipe and ordering another round of white wine; I don't quite remember what I felt at giving up my impulse, but it was something like prohibition, the feeling that if I defied it I would enter unsure territory. And still I think I did wrong; I was on the verge of an act that would have saved me. Saved me from what? I wonder. But precisely that: saved me from being able only to wonder about it today, and from having no other answer than tobacco smoke and this vague futile hope that follows me on the streets like a mangy dog.

> *Où sont-ils passés, les becs de gaz? Que*
> *sont-elles devenues, les vendeuses d'amour?*
> ...., VI, 1.

Little by little I had to convince myself that we had come into bad times and that while Laurent and the Prussian menace worried us that way, life in the galleries would never go back to being what it had been. My mother must have noticed I was depressed, because she advised me to take some tonic, and Irma's parents, who had a chalet on an island in the Paraná, invited me to spend some time there, resting and leading a healthy life. I asked for fifteen days vacation and left unwillingly for the island, enemies from the start with the sun and mosquitoes. The first Saturday, I made up any old pretext and returned to the city; I stumbled along streets where heels sank into the soft asphalt. Of that senseless vagrancy remains a sudden delicious memory: As I entered the Güemes Arcade once again, the aroma of coffee suddenly enfolded me, its violence already almost forgotten in galleries where the coffee was weak and reheated. I drank two cups, without sugar, tasting and smelling at the same time, scalding myself and happy. All that came after, until the afternoon's end, smelled different—the humid downtown air was full of pockets of fragrance (I returned home on foot, I believe I had promised my mother to dine with her), and in each pocket of air the smells were more raw, more intense—yellow soap, coffee, black tobacco, printing ink, bitter maté, everything smelled pitilessly, and the sun and sky, too, were harder and more urgent. For some hours, I almost begrudgingly forgot the gallery district, but when I again crossed the Güemes Arcade (was it really at the time of the island? Perhaps I am confusing two moments of the same period, it hardly matters, really), it was fruitless to invoke the jolly slap of the coffee. Its smell seemed the same as always, and instead I recognized that sweetish, repugnant mixture of sawdust and stale beer that seems to ooze from the floors of downtown bars, but perhaps it was because, again, I wanted to find Josiane and I even trusted in the fact that the great terror and the snows had reached their end. I think it was in those days that I began to suspect that desire wasn't enough, as before, for things to revolve rhythmically and suggest some of the streets that led to the Galerie Vivienne, but it's also possible that I ended up giving in meekly to the chalet on the island so as not to make Irma sad, so she wouldn't suspect that my only true repose was elsewhere; until I couldn't stand it any longer and went back to the city and walked until I was exhausted, with my shirt sticking to my body, sitting in the bars drinking beer, waiting for I no longer knew what. And when, on leaving the last bar, I saw that I had only to turn the corner to enter my neighborhood, happiness and fatigue and a dark consciousness of failure became one, because it was enough to look into people's faces to realize that the great terror was far from over, it was enough to look into Josiane's eyes on her corner on the Rue d'Uzès and hear her grumble that the boss had decided to protect her personally from a possible attack; I remember that between two kisses I managed to get a glimpse of his figure in the hollow of a doorway, protecting himself from the sleet with a long gray cape.

Josiane was not the kind to resent absences, and I wonder if she was really aware of the passage of time. We returned arm in arm to the Galerie Vivienne, we went up to the garret, but later we realized we weren't happy as before and we vaguely attributed it to all that was upsetting the neighborhood; there would be war, it was inevitable, the men would have to join the ranks (she used these words solemnly, with an ignorant, delightful respect), the people were afraid and angry, the police had been unable to find Laurent. They consoled themselves by guillotining others— that very morning, for instance, they'd execute the poisoner of whom we'd spoken so much in the Rue des Jeûneurs café during the days of the trial, but the terror was still loose in the galleries and arcades; nothing had changed since the last time I saw Josiane, and it hadn't even stopped snowing.

As a consolation, we went for a walk, defying the cold, because Josiane had a coat which had to be admired on a series of corners and doorways where her friends were wait- ing for customers, blowing on their fingers or sticking their hands into their fur muffs. Seldom had we taken such a long walk along the boulevards, and I ended up suspecting that, above all, we were sensitive to the protection of the lighted show windows; venturing into any of the nearby streets (because Liliane had to see the coat, too, and further on Francine) sank us further and further into alarm, until the coat had been sufficiently exhibited, and I suggested our café, and we ran along the Rue de Croissant until turning the corner and taking refuge in warmth and among our friends. Luckily for all, the idea of war at that hour was dim in people's memories. Nobody thought of repeating the obscene refrains against the Prussians, everything was so good with the full glasses and the brazier's heat and only we, the owner's friends, were left, yes, the same group as always and the good news that La Rousse had apologized to Josiane and that they had made up with kisses and tears and even gifts. It all had a garland quality (but garlands can be funereal, I understood afterwards) and that's why, with the snow and Laurent outside, we stayed as long as we could in the café and found out at midnight that it was the owner's fiftieth anniversary of working behind the same counter, and this had to be celebrated. One flower intertwined with the next, and bottles filled the tables, because now the owner was treating everybody, and you couldn't slight such friendship and such dedication to work, and around three-thirty in the morning Kiki, completely drunk, ended up singing the best airs of the operettas of the day, while Josiane and La Rousse cried in each other's arms out of happiness and absinthe, and Albert, almost without giving it importance, twined another flower in the garland and suggested ending the night at La Roquette, where they would guillotine the poisoner at six o'clock sharp, and the owner, extremely moved, realized that the party's end was like the apotheosis of fifty years of honorable work and he insisted, embracing us all and telling us about his dead wife in Languedoc, upon renting two hackney coaches for the expedition.

After that, more wine followed, the evocation of several mothers and outstanding childhood episodes, and an onion soup that Josiane and La Rousse raised to the sublime in the kitchen, while Albert, the owner, and I swore eternal friendship and death to the Prussians. The soup and cheeses must have drowned such vehemence, because we were all almost quiet and even uncomfortable when the moment came to close the café with an endless noise of bars and chains, and to climb into the hackney coaches where all the cold in the world seemed to be waiting for us. It would have been better for us to travel together to keep warm, but the owner had humanitarian principles when it came to horses, and he got into the first carriage with La Rousse and Albert, while he entrusted me with Kiki and Josiane, who, he said, were like daughters to him. After these words had been toasted to the full with the coach drivers, the spirit returned to our bodies as we rode toward Popincourt amid mock racing, shouts of encouragement, and a rain of false whippings. The owner insisted upon getting off at a certain distance, citing reasons of discretion which I didn't understand, and arm in arm, so as not to slip on the frozen snow, we walked up the Rue de la Roquette, vaguely lit by occasional gaslight, among moving shadows which suddenly materialized into top hats, trotting coaches, and groups of cloaked figures gathering finally in front of a wide end of the street, beneath the other taller and blacker shadow of the jail. A secret world clinked elbows, passed bottles from hand to hand, repeated a joke that ran through boisterous laughter and choked shrieks, and there were also sudden silences and faces lit for a moment by a match, while we kept pushing ahead, being careful not to separate, as if each knew that only the will of the group could pardon its presence in that place. The machine was there on its five stone bases, and the whole apparatus of justice waited motionless in the brief space between it and the square body of soldiers with their rifles resting on the ground and fixed bayonets. Josiane stuck her nails into my arm and trembled in such a way that I spoke of taking her to a café, but there were no cafés in sight, and she insisted upon staying. Hanging on me and Albert, she jumped from time to time to get a better view of the machine, stuck her nails in me again, and finally made me stoop my head until her lips found my mouth and bit me hysterically, murmuring words I'd seldom heard her say and which boosted my pride, as if for a moment I had been the boss. But of all of us the only real *aficionado* was Albert; smoking a cigar, he killed the minutes comparing ceremonies, imagining the condemned man's final behavior, the stages which in that moment were taking place inside the prison and which he knew in detail for reasons he didn't say. At first, I listened eagerly to learn about each and every part of the liturgy, until slowly, as from beyond him and Josiane and the celebration of the anniversary, something like abandon gradually came over me, the indefinable feeling that this shouldn't happen in this way, that something was threatening the world of the galleries and arcades in me, or still worse, that my happiness in that world had been a deceptive prelude, a snare of flowers, as if one of the plaster figures had offered me a false garland (and I had thought that night how things were woven like the flowers on a garland), to little by little fall back to Laurent, to turn away from the innocent intoxication of the Galerie Vivienne and Josiane's garret, slowly moving toward the great terror, the snow, the inevitable war, the apotheosis of the owner's fifty years, the frozen-stiff hackney coaches of dawn, the tense arm of Josiane, who swore she wouldn't look and who was already seeking a place on my chest to hide her face in the final moment. It seemed (and in that moment the gates began to open, and you could hear the commanding voice of the officer of the guard) that somehow this was an end—I wasn't sure of what, because after all I would keep on living, working in the stock market, occasionally seeing Josiane, Albert, and Kiki, who was now beating my shoulder hysterically, and although I didn't want to take my eyes off the gates that were just opening, I had to give her some attention for a moment, and following her at once surprised and mocking stare, I glimpsed almost beside the owner the slightly bent figure of the South American in a black student gown, and curiously I thought that, too, entered into the garland somehow, and it was a little as if a hand had just woven in the flower that would close it before daybreak. And then I didn't think anymore, because Josiane pressed against me moaning, and in the shadow which the two gaslights beside the door wavered without driving it away, the white spot of a shirt appeared, floating between two black figures, appearing and disappearing each time a third bulky shadow bent over it with the gestures of a person embracing or advising or saying something in someone's ear or giving him something to kiss, until it moved to one side, and the white spot became clearer, closer, framed by a group of people in top hats and black coats, and there was a sort of accelerated magic trick, an abduction of the white spot by two figures, which, until that moment, had seemed to form part of the machine, a motion of pulling from someone's shoulders a now unnecessary coat, a hurried movement forward, someone's muffled outcry, maybe Josiane's, convulsing against me, maybe from the white spot, which seemed to slide under the framework, where something was unchained with an almost simultaneous cracking and commotion. I thought that Josiane was going to faint; all the weight of her body slipped down mine as the other body must have been slipping toward nothingness, and I stooped to hold her up while an enormous knot of throats unwound in a Mass finale, with the organ resounding on high (but it was a horse that neighed on smelling blood), and the ebbing crowd pushed us amid the military shouting of orders. Over Josiane's hat—she was now crying mercifully against my stomach—I had a glimpse of the excited café owner, Albert, in his glory, and the profile of the South American lost in the imperfect contemplation of the machine, which soldiers' backs and over-zealous craftsmen of justice occasionally revealed, in lightning bolts of shadow between arms and overcoats and a general eagerness to move on in search of hot wine and sleep, like ourselves later piling into a coach to go back, remarking on what each thought he had seen, which was not the same, was never the same, and that's why it was worth more, because between the Rue de la Roquette and the stock exchange district there was time to reconstruct the ceremony, discuss it, catch yourself at contradictions, brag about sharper sight or steadier nerves to the last-minute admiration of our timid companions.

It was not at all strange that in those days my mother found me worse and outspokenly complained of this puzzling indifference which made my poor fiancée suffer and would end up by depriving me of my deceased father's friends' protection, thanks to which I was making my way in stock exchange circles. The only answer to such words was silence, and to come home a few days later with a new plant or a discount coupon for skeins of wool. Irma was more understanding. She must simply have counted on marriage to one day bring me back to bureaucratic normality, and in those last times I was on the verge of agreeing with her, but it was impossible for me to give up the hope that the great terror would come to its end in the gallery district and that going home would no longer seem an escape, a need for protection which would disappear as soon as my mother would look at me sighing or Irma would serve me coffee with the fiancée spider smile. We were then under military dictatorship in Argentina, one more in the endless series, but the people were excited above all about the imminent outcome of the world war, and almost everyday they had demonstrations downtown to celebrate the Allied advance and the liberation of the European capitals, while the police charged against students and women, stores hurriedly lowered their metal curtains and I, incorporated by the force of things into some group standing in front of the bulletin boards of *La Prensa*, wondered how much longer I could stand poor Irma's inevitable smile and the dampness that soaked my shirt between sessions of quotations. I began to feel that the gallery district was no longer the limit of a desire, as before, when it was enough to walk down any street for everything to revolve softly on any corner, so that I'd effortlessly reach the Place des Victoires, where it was so pleasing to browse around the side streets with their dusty stores and entrance-ways and, at the most propitious hour, enter the Galerie Vivienne in search of Josiane, unless I'd whimsically prefer to first take in the Passage des Panoramas or the Passage des Princes and return by way of a slightly perverse detour around the stock exchange. Now, instead, without even the consolation of recognizing, as on that morning, the fierce smell of coffee in the Güemes Arcade (it smelled of sawdust, of lye), I began to admit from way back that the gallery district was no longer the port of repose, although I still believed in the possibility of breaking away from my work and Irma, of effortlessly finding Josiane's corner. The desire to return was constantly alluring me; in front of the newspapers' bulletin boards, with my friends, at home in the patio, especially at dusk, when there they'd be turning on the gaslights. But something made me stay with my mother and Irma, a dark certainty that they would not wait for me as before in the gallery district, that the great terror was stronger. I'd walk into the banks and places of business like an automation, tolerating my daily obligation to buy and sell stocks, listening to the hoofs of police horses charging against the people who were celebrating the Allied victories, and so little did I now believe that I could free myself from all this that when I got to the gallery district I was almost afraid. I felt like a stranger and different than ever before, I took refuge in a doorway and let people and time pass, forced for the first time to accept bit by bit all that had seemed to be mine before—streets and vehicles, clothes and gloves, snow in the patios, and voices in the stores. Until again it was wonderment; it was finding Josiane in the Gal-

erie Colbert and finding out between kisses and leaps that
Laurent no longer was, that the whole neighborhood had
celebrated the nightmare's end night after night, and everybody had asked for me and a good thing that Laurent finally
. . . but where had I been that I didn't know anything about
it, and so many things, and so many kisses. Never had I
wanted her more and never did we love each other better
beneath the ceiling of her room that my hand could touch
from the bed. The caresses, the gossip, the delicious inventory of the days, while twilight gradually came over the
room. Laurent? A curly-haired Marseillais, a miserable cow-
ard who had barricaded himself in the loft of the house,
where he had just killed another woman, and desperately
had begged for mercy while the police knocked the door
down. And his name was Paul, the monster, imagine that,
and he had just killed his ninth victim, and they had dragged
him to the police van while the whole force of the second
district halfheartedly protected him from a crowd that
would have torn him to shreds. Josiane already had time to
get used to it, to bury Laurent in her memory, which seldom
retained images, but for me it was too much, and I couldn't
believe it until her joy finally convinced me that there really
would be no more Laurent, that we could wander again
through the arcades and streets without distrusting doorways. We would have to go out and celebrate the Liberation
together, and as it was not snowing now, Josiane wanted to
go to the Palais-Royal Rotunda, which we had never fre-
quented in the times of Laurent. I promised myself, while
we went singing down the Rue des Petits Champs, that that
same night I would take Josiane to the boulevard cabarets,
and that we would finish the evening in our café, where,
with the help of white wine, I would make all forgive me for
such ingratitude and absence.

For a few hours, I drank down the happy time of the

galleries, and I became convinced that the end of the great terror would make me healthy and happy again under my sky of stucco and garlands; dancing with Josiane in the Rotunda, I threw off the last oppression of that uncertain interval, I was born again into my better life, so far from Irma's drawing room, the patio at home, the deficient consolation of the Güemes Arcade. Not even later, when, chatting about so many happy things with Kiki and Josiane and the café owner, I learned about the last of the South American, not even then did I suspect that I was living on borrowed time, a last grace; besides, they talked about the South American with a mocking indifference, as if about any of the neighborhood's oddballs, who managed to fill a gap in a conversation where soon more exciting subjects would be born; that the South American had just died in a hotel room was scarcely anything more than some information in passing, and Kiki was already discussing the parties being prepared in a *moulin* on La Butte, and it was hard work interrupting her, asking for some detail, hardly knowing why I asked. Through Kiki, I found out some minor things—the South American's name, which after all was a French name, and which I forgot immediately, his sudden illness on the Rue du Faubourg Montmartre, where Kiki had a friend who had told her; his loneliness, the one measly taper burning on the shelves full of books and papers, the gray cat that her friend had picked up, the anger of the hotel manager, to whom they did those things precisely when he was expecting a visit from his in-laws, the anonymous burial, oblivion, the parties in the *moulin* on la Butte, the arrest of Paul the Marseillais, the insolence of the Prussians, for whom the time was ripe to give them a lesson they deserved. And out of all that I separated, like one who pulls two dry flowers off a garland, the two deaths which somehow seemed in my eyes symmetrical, the South American's and Laurent's, the one in his hotel room, the other dissolving into nothingness to yield his place to Paul the Marseillais, and they were almost the same death, something erased forever in the neighborhood's memory. That night, I could still believe that everything would continue as before the great terror, and Josiane was again mine in her garret, and when saying goodnight we promised each other parties and excursions when summer arrived. But it was freezing in the streets, and the news of the war required my presence at the stock exchange at nine in the morning; with an effort which I then thought commendable, I refused to think about my reconquered heaven, and after working till dizzy I lunched with my mother and thanked her for finding me in better form. I spent that week immersed in stock exchange struggles with no time for anything, running home to take a shower and changing one soaked shirt for another, which in a while was worse. The bomb fell on Hiroshima, and all was confusion among my customers, I had to wage a long battle to save the most committed stocks and to find an advisable direction in that world where each day was a new Nazi defeat and the dictatorship's angry, futile reaction against the irretrievable. When the Germans surrendered, and the people filled the streets of Buenos Aires, I thought I could take a rest, but each morning new problems awaited me: In those weeks, I married Irma after my mother was on the verge of a heart attack, which the whole family blamed me for, perhaps rightly so. Time and again, I wondered why, if the great terror had ended in the gallery district, the moment never came for me to meet Josiane and again take walks beneath our plaster heaven. I suppose work and family obligations contributed to keeping me from it, and I only know that at odd moments I would take a walk along the Güemes Arcade as a consolation, looking vaguely up, drinking coffee and thinking, each time with less conviction, of the afternoons when I had only to wander a while, without fixed destination, to get to my neighborhood and meet up with Josiane on some corner of twilight. I have never wanted to admit that the garland was closed definitively and that I would not meet Josiane again in the arcades and on the boulevards. Some days I get to thinking about the South American, and in that halfhearted rumination I invent a sort of consolation, as if he had killed Laurent and myself with his own death; sensibly I tell myself no, I'm exaggerating, any day now I'll again venture into the gallery district and find Josiane surprised by my long absence. And between one thing and another I stay home drinking maté, listening to Irma, who's expecting in December, and wonder, not too enthusiastically, if at election time I'll vote for Perón or for Tamborini, if I'll vote none of the above and simply stay home drinking maté and looking at Irma and the plants in the patio.

PANTHEON MODERN WRITERS ORIGINALS

THE VICE-CONSUL
by Marguerite Duras, translated from the French by Eileen Ellenbogen

The first American edition ever of the novel Marguerite Duras considers her best—a tale of passion and desperation set in India and Southeast Asia.

"A masterful novel."—*The Chicago Tribune*
0-394-55898-7 cloth, $10.95   0-394-75026-8 paper, $6.95

MAPS
by Nuruddin Farah

The unforgettable story of one man's coming of age in the turmoil of modern Africa.

"A true and rich work of art . . . [by] one of the finest contemporary African writers."
—Salman Rushdie
0-394-56325-5 cloth, $11.95   0-394-75548-0 paper, $7.95

DREAMING JUNGLES
by Michel Rio, translated from the French by William Carlson

A hypnotic novel about an elegant French scientist and his shattering confrontation in turn-of-the-century Africa with the jungle, passion, and at last, himself.

"A subtle philosophical excursion embodied in a story of travel and adventure. . . . It succeeds extremely well."   —*The New York Times Book Review*
0-394-55661-5 cloth, $10.95   0-394-75035-7 paper, $6.95

BURNING PATIENCE
by Antonio Skármeta, translated from the Spanish by Katherine Silver

A charming story about the friendship that develops between Pablo Neruda, Latin America's greatest poet, and the postman who stops to receive his advice about love.

"The mix of the fictional and the real is masterful, and . . . gives the book its special appeal and brilliance."   —*Christian Science Monitor*
0-394-55576-7 cloth, $10.95   0-394-75033-0 paper, $6.95

YOU CAN'T GET LOST IN CAPE TOWN
by Zoë Wicomb

Nine stories powerfully evoke a young black woman's upbringing in South Africa.

"A superb first collection."—*The New York Times Book Review*
0-394-56030-2 cloth, $10.95   0-394-75309-7 paper, $6.95

THE SHOOTING GALLERY
by Yūko Tsushima, compiled and translated from the Japanese by Geraldine Harcourt

Eight stories about modern Japanese women by one of Japan's finest contemporary writers.

"Tsushima is a subtle, surprising, elegant writer who courageously tells unexpected truths."   —Margaret Drabble
0-394-75743-2 paper, $7.95

THE WINNERS

by Julio Cortázar, translated from the Spanish by Elaine Kerrigan

Julio Cortázar's superb first novel about a South American luxury cruise.

"Irresistibly readable . . . introduces a dazzling writer."
— *The New York Times Book Review*
0-394-72301-5 paper, $8.95

THE LEOPARD

by Giuseppe di Lampedusa, translated from the Italian by Archibald Colquhoun

The world-renowned novel of a Sicilian prince in the turbulent Italy of the 1860s.

"The genius of its author and the thrill it gives the reader are probably for all time."
— *The New York Times Book Review*
0-394-74949-9 paper, $7.95

YOUNG TÖRLESS

by Robert Musil, translated from the German
by Eithne Williams and Ernst Kaiser

A classic novel by the author of *The Man Without Qualities,* about students at an Austrian military academy and their brutality to one another.

"An illumination of the dark places of the heart." — *The Washington Post*
0-394-71015-0 paper, $6.95

ADIEUX: A FAREWELL TO SARTRE

by Simone de Beauvoir, translated from the French by Patrick O'Brian

Simone de Beauvoir's moving farewell to Jean-Paul Sartre: "an intimate, personal, and honest portrait of a relationship unlike any other in literary history." —Deirdre Bair
0-394-72898-X paper, $8.95

THE BLOOD OF OTHERS

by Simone de Beauvoir,
translated from the French by Roger Senhouse and Yvonne Moyse

A brilliant existentialist novel about the French resistance, "with a remarkably sustained note of suspense and mounting excitement." — *Saturday Review*
0-394-72411-9 paper, $7.95

A VERY EASY DEATH

by Simone de Beauvoir, translated from the French by Patrick O'Brian

The profoundly moving, day-by-day account of the death of the author's mother.

"A beautiful book, sincere and sensitive." — Pierre-Henri Simon
0-394-72899-8 paper, $4.95

WHEN THINGS OF THE SPIRIT COME FIRST: FIVE EARLY TALES

by Simone de Beauvoir, translated from the French by Patrick O'Brian

The first paperback edition of the marvelous early fiction of Simone de Beauvoir.

"An event for celebration." — *The New York Times Book Review*
0-394-72235-3 paper, $6.95

Ask at Your Local Bookstore for Other Pantheon Modern Writers Titles.